Poplar Falls

The Death of Charlie Baker

ISBN: 978-1-932926-68-2
LCCN: 2018908332
Copyright © 2019 by Pierre C. Arseneault

Cover Design: Angella Cormier
Cover Photo: Pierre C. Arseneault
Author Photo: Gerard Gaudet

Artemesia Publishing
9 Mockingbird Hill Rd
Tijeras, New Mexico 87059
www.apbooks.net
info@artemesiapublishing.com

Poplar Falls

The Death of Charlie Baker

by

Pierre C. Arseneault

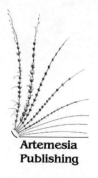

Artemesia
Publishing

Other titles by Pierre C. Arseneault are:

Dark Tales for Dark Nights, a collection of six short stories written in collaboration with Angella Jacob (Cormier).
Sleepless Nights, a collection of nine short stories.
Oakwood Island, a novel written in collaboration with Angella Cormier.

This book is for all those who told me they didn't like reading scary books. This one's for you.

Are addictions holding you back, hurting those you love and affecting your career? Do you suffer from an addiction to drugs, alcohol, or sex? The dedicated and highly-trained staff at the Magnolia Wellness and Rehabilitation Centre are here to help you get your life back on track.

Our services include counselling with licensed therapists and access to amazing support groups. All of this is provided while staying at the serene and relaxing Magnolia estate, which is nestled on the outskirts of the small and beautiful city of Poplar Falls, filled with small-town charm and surrounded by the relaxing splendor of rivers and picturesque waterfalls.

Come stay a while and let us help you.

Stella P. Rubbin
Magnolia Wellness and Rehabilitation Centre Manager

June

1

Standing at the foot of the bed, a salt-and-pepper-haired Senior Detective Franklin Dodge elbowed his partner as if to say, *Look at that.* The much younger Detective Roxanne Tilley just stared on in disbelief.

"I didn't think that was possible," Detective Tilley said in a hushed tone while shifting her stance a little. Her facial expression was riddled with embarrassment, which her dark skin somewhat hid from her partner, who was clearly observing her reaction. She shifted uncomfortably and tugged at the collar of her white blouse under the grey feminine suit jacket.

"I guess it is," Dodge replied, sounding unsure even though the evidence stood before them. He wore faded jeans with a battered suit jacket and his face was flushed. He tugged at his shirt collar and loosened his tie a little in an attempt to cool off. The hot June morning sun shone through the sheer curtains, making the room warm, but under the circumstances it felt even warmer, as being uncomfortably embarrassed can have that effect on anyone.

On the bed before them lay the naked body of one Charlie Baker. Spread-eagled, flat on his back, with hands and legs bound with heavy silk ropes to the metal four-post bed frame. His torso was concealed under a thin, off-white silk blanket. His Caucasian skin had the grey hue of death to it. A crumpled pillow rested on his face, making it obvious that he had been smothered to death while he tugged at his bonds. Rigor mortis had set in before they found him, and Charlie was as stiff as a piece of mahogany. Every inch of him was stiff, from head to toe, including his much larger than average penis, which was creating an unusually large tent out of the thin silk blanket.

"You mind telling me why this Agatha called you directly instead of calling 911?" Dodge asked as he glanced at Tilley before turning back to the uncomfortable scene before them.

"I thought I told you already," Detective Tilley replied. "She's my great-aunt on my mother's side."

"Right," Dodge replied. He often forgot that Roxanne's mother was white. Her dark brown skin was from her father. And while he knew of the older landlady from his original stint at apartment hunting before he purchased a house, he didn't know that Agatha was related to Tilley. He made a mental note to ask her about that later. "The murder just happens to be at your great-aunt's place," he said, smirking. "That's great!"

"She owns apartments all over town," Detective Tilley replied, and she smiled smugly, as if the great detective should have known this. "I think you forget that I'm from Poplar Falls."

"True enough," Dodge replied. He hadn't forgotten that Tilley was from Poplar Falls; how could he? It seemed like she knew everybody from this little city. He turned his attention from the body on the bed and looked around the apartment. It was large for a one-room, open-concept bachelor pad. Big curtained windows let in much of the summer sunlight, but the sheer curtains weren't enough to provide privacy, thought Dodge. The only other room was a good-sized bathroom at the back of the apartment which they had checked upon entering to ensure no one else was there. The apartment was messy, for the most part, with clean and dirty clothes strewn about on the floor as well as draped over the furniture. Empty food containers sat in various strange locations around the apartment. A stack of dirty containers sat on and underneath a kitchen chair, as if he had gathered some in a pile. The kitchenette's counter wasn't visible under the mess of even more food containers, dirty dishes, and casserole dishes. Dodge had the sneaking suspicion that those casserole dishes weren't Charlie's.

On a small kitchen table were porn magazines and DVDs of the same genre. Charlie wasn't very discreet, Dodge reflected. He assumed that Charlie might have had company often enough, as it was obvious no woman lived here, yet on the floor were a pair of women's shoes, size six or seven from the looks of them. He glanced at the body and back to the shoes and assessed that they were too small to belong to Charlie. Sexy red heels. Plus, some of the casserole dishes where too big for the microwave, and the apartment had no oven in its kitchenette.

"Lemkie and Calvin should be here later this morning," Tilley said, referring to the Poplar Falls crime scene investigators. She was still mesmerized by the scene before her and hadn't moved from the foot of the bed. Neither had Dodge.

Dodge turned to look at his partner again and cleared his throat before speaking. "Did you ask her yet?"

"We just got here *maybe* ten minutes ago," Roxanne replied. "What I wonder is how the hell anyone is going to make sense out of anything in this mess."

Dodge pointed to the nightstand. "That explains the tent pole."

Tilley finally pulled her eyes away from said tent pole where she had been staring, fascinated by the shape of the large tip. Her attention went to the half-empty bottle of pills which sat precariously perched on the edge of the nightstand.

At that very moment, the doorbell rang and startled both detectives. The bell-like chime rang a second time, resonating throughout the small apartment. The detectives glanced at each other in confusion. They hadn't shut the door but remembered hearing it close behind them as they had entered. Perhaps a draft had closed it, thought Dodge as he shrugged and gestured for Tilley to take the lead.

"What if it's the killer?" Tilley asked with an obvious air of sarcasm.

"Really?" Dodge replied with a grin as he played along. "I doubt the killer would bother with the doorbell."

With a hand on the butt of her gun, Tilley peered through the peephole in the solid wooden door. Glancing back at Dodge with apparent confusion on her face, she moved her hand from her gun to the doorknob. Dodge put his hand on hers to stop her and then pulled back. He had only recently begun to trust his young partner's instincts, but old habits die hard. Tilley didn't bother to unlock the deadbolt. A broken piece of the doorframe still clung to the hardware as she opened the door. This was courtesy of Dodge's now-sore shoulder.

2

Detective Tilley opened the door to see a woman she knew well, standing outside on the second-floor balcony in the morning sunlight. The woman's gaze was cast down as she fiddled nervously with her long, beige overcoat. Before anyone could say anything the woman flung open the coat, revealing a very skimpy, lace-trimmed, blue teddy which barely covered her curvaceous body. A look of shock washed over all three of them as the woman realized she had flashed someone other than the intended Charlie Baker. Dodge's mouth was slightly agape as he took in the curvy woman's private peepshow clearly not intended for them.

"Ms. Weatherbee!" Detective Tilley exclaimed in shock.

The clearly-embarrassed woman closed the overcoat tightly around her body. Her face flushed a deep red with humiliation as she spun around and sprinted off the stoop, down the steps. The shocked detectives stood speechless at first.

"Wait!" Dodge shouted, but it was too late as the woman jumped into a small blue hatchback and drove away. He turned to his partner and asked, "You know her?"

"That was my fifth-grade teacher," Detective Tilley replied.

"I wish my fifth-grade teacher had looked like that," Dodge replied. "Puberty would have been a much different experience for me." Dodge had a flash of memory of old, crusty, grey-haired Mr. Martin, his fifth-grade teacher, and shuddered at the thought.

They watched the car disappear as it rounded a corner at breakneck speed, just in time to avoid the oncoming police cruiser—the first one to arrive on the scene.

"It's okay," Tilley replied. "I know where she lives."

Dodge started chuckling at the whole thing while Tilley tried to remain serious but failed. Everyone in town, including his partner at times, still treated him like he had just moved here, even though it had been over two years already. He considered this a good thing since knowing too much about someone you might be investigating can alter your perception. But he would never tell his partner this since she was from Poplar Falls, and was convinced that knowing people well would make her a better detective. But right at this moment he wouldn't even admit to himself that he was glad she was a local since she knew this Ms. Weatherbee

3

Two hours later, the large gravel parking lot was surrounded by yellow police tape, an obvious crime scene to all who happened by, which meant rumours were now rampant all over town and on social media. A small crowd had gathered to try and catch a glimpse of what was going on so they could spread the gossip. A few reporters had joined the crowd and everybody was snapping pictures and taking video with their smartphones. Many were already posting pictures on Facebook and Twitter for the entire world to see, hoping for their videos to go viral.

Dodge climbed out of his old, rusty Ford Escape with a tray of coffees. He handed them to the paramedics who were waiting outside by their ambulance. Clearly, they had assessed that they were not needed here, as Charlie was long dead. "The captain's gonna love this," Tilley said to Dodge as she examined the growing throng of spectators.

Dodge handed a coffee to Tilley and took the last one as he glanced around to make sure nobody could overhear them.

"Did you have a chance to ask her about the key to the deadbolt yet?" Dodge inquired.

"Yes, although I didn't really get to talk to her much," Tilley replied.

"So?" Dodge asked as he sipped coffee.

"She didn't seem to know about it," Tilley said. "I'm pretty sure it's something Charlie installed himself."

"That would explain why Agatha only gave you a key for the door handle and not the deadbolt," Dodge replied. "But that doesn't explain how she knew he was dead if she didn't have a key to get into his place."

"True," Detective Tilley replied knowingly. "And she did say he was dead and not in trouble when she called me." Tilley sipped her coffee. "Dead was definitely the word she used."

Dodge turned back and watched the crime scene investigators arriving, which caused a flurry of rubberneckers to lift their smartphones and take more pictures. Dodge scanned the crowd and recognized a few familiar faces.

"You know much about this Charlie Baker?" Dodge

asked.

"From what my aunt told me, he always paid his rent in cash and had only been living in town for seven months."

Dodge grinned as he spoke. "For a sweet old lady, she looked pissed when Roger took her in."

Tilley couldn't help but smile at the thought and then looked around to see if anyone had seen her do so. Worse, had they taken her picture? Perhaps even filming them, taking video.

"I figured it best if a patrolman took her in instead of me. Since she's my aunt and all," Tilley said.

"Yeah," Dodge replied. "Best to play it safe, but somehow I doubt she's our killer."

Detective Tilley laughed, covering her mouth with the back of her hand, and looked around to see if anyone had heard her, especially those reporters.

4

Hours later, both detectives stood next to the bathroom door of Charlie Baker's apartment as they watched the lead crime scene investigator, Lemkie, bagging what looked like used tampons from the bathroom floor next to the trashcan. Once that was done, he carefully slid the trashcan and all its contents into a large bag and sealed it shut.

"I'm not taking any chances," Lemkie stated. "There might be something in there that's important."

"Did you see how many condom wrappers were in that trashcan?" Tilley asked.

"His sex life was better than mine," Dodge remarked.

"Yours, mine, and Tilley's combined," Lemkie replied.

"Well, you're married," Dodge said to Lemkie. "Yours is over."

"Yeah, no comment," Tilley murmured.

Dodge glanced at her with a knowing smile. At least he thought he knew since he lived across the street from Tilley and never saw any other vehicles at her place. Although she could say the same thing about him, as he also never had visitors. But she didn't need to know about his friend who lived within walking distance.

"You wanted to see us?" Dodge asked, trying to get back on track.

"I wanted to show you this," Lemkie replied as he led the detectives out of the washroom. They walked past crime scene investigator Calvin, the one a lot of people still referred to as the new kid, even though he'd been there almost as long as Dodge. He was in the process of cutting and bagging the silk ropes that had held Charlie in place while he was murdered.

Lemkie led the detectives to a shelf against a wall while he spoke. "When you told me that the door was locked with a deadbolt and Agatha didn't have a key to give you, I wondered how she could have known he was lying here dead."

"We were wondering that ourselves," Dodge said, subconsciously rubbing the tender shoulder he'd used to bash in the door.

"Well, I remembered you saying she lived next door." Lemkie took a pen from his pocket and moved a cheap painting of a landscape aside to better reveal what he had discovered. Between the shelf and the painting was a small peephole, not much bigger than the pen Lemkie was holding.

"I guess that explains how Aunt Agatha knew Charlie was dead," Dodge said, and he smirked and glanced at his partner who was flustered with embarrassment. After all, Aunt Agatha lived in the apartment next door to Charlie and the peephole had to be hers.

"Sure," Lemkie replied. "But that's nothing. Check this out." Using his pen again, he pointed to a book on the shelf. He pointed to a black circle and looked at Tilley, anticipating a reaction as he explained what was obvious to him. "It's a camera."

"Well, now—Aunt Agatha's full of surprises," Dodge said.

"No," Lemkie replied. "Not Agatha. These were his. They had to be."

Lemkie walked past Calvin, who had stopped what he was doing and was watching them intensely. Lemkie pointed to a bizarre statue of a rabbit that was perched atop the television on a stand in a corner.

Dodge laughed abruptly and everyone glared at him.

"Rabbit ears for better reception," Dodge said, which made Calvin scratch his head and Tilley smile. Lemkie ignored him. This reminded Dodge how much older than everyone else he was and his grin quickly vanished.

"Another camera," Lemkie said.

"Are they on now?" Tilley asked.

"I don't think so," Calvin replied.

Everyone looked at Calvin as he explained. "I think they're wireless cameras, but my bet is they fed to a laptop or something," he said as he pointed to a blank space on a shelf. A small remote still sat there but what they assumed was a laptop, from the shape of the dusty imprint, was gone. And the lack of dust in the imprint suggested it had been removed very recently.

"I figure we're going to find more of those," Calvin added as he went back to collecting the other rope from stiff Charlie's other leg. Everyone couldn't help but glance over at the large tent pole still standing at attention.

"Tell them what you told me," Lemkie said to Calvin.

Calvin set himself to cutting the rope, being careful not to remove any potential evidence in the process as he spoke, obviously avoiding eye contact.

"Charlie here used to make porn," Calvin murmured.

"He what?" Dodge asked.

"How do you..." Tilley started asking, and then decided

she really didn't want to know.

"Well, he used to, anyway," Calvin stated with a little more confidence in his voice than his previous statement. "He used to post videos to a website I might have heard of; up until about a year ago anyway, more or less."

"Well now, the late Charlie here is turning into some sort of sex fiend," Dodge said. "This is gonna be one for the books. I can already see that."

Lemkie and Calvin positioned themselves on each side of the bed and slowly lifted the silk blanket, exposing what it had hidden up until then.

"Holy torpedo," Dodge said.

Tilley gasped.

Lemkie muttered something nobody understood.

5

"Well, that was interesting," Dodge said, lifting the yellow police tape to scoot under it. He held it up as his partner followed.

"Yeah," Tilley replied. "But I don't think we're going to get anywhere with any of the DNA or prints they're going to collect in there."

"Well at least we might have a list of potential suspects. This might end up being a process of elimination type of thing," Dodge replied as he pointed to something away from the crime scene.

Tilley followed her partner's gaze to a small but neat bungalow. Almost directly across the road sat a little white house with a covered porch and elaborate landscape consisting of many flowerbeds, bushes, and shrubberies.

"We might as well start with them," Dodge said, clearly meaning the elderly couple sitting on the covered porch.

"That's Mr. and Mrs. O'Brien," Tilley said. "He's a retired

pen salesman and she was his secretary, until his wife caught them having an affair. They got married after his divorce was final."

"Every time I forget, you blurt out someone's entire life's history to remind me you're from Poplar Falls."

"I don't know everybody," Tilley replied defensively. "But Emma and Agatha are friends. That, and the O'Briens babysat me and my sisters when we were little."

Dodge stuck out a hand to stop a car that had been creeping by while gawking at the crime scene. As they crossed the street, they could see Mrs. O'Brien wave her arm around as she peeked over her glasses at them. She was holding a cordless telephone to her ear with her other hand. She waved again as if she was swatting at pesky flies or something. Mr. O'Brien sat next to her peering through a rather large pair of binoculars. Emma tugged at her husband's elbow as she watched the detectives approach.

"What?" Bill barked as he lowered his binoculars and squinted to see who approached. He grasped clumsily at the thick glasses hanging on a string around his neck and put them on.

"I gotta go," Emma said as she pushed buttons on her cordless phone while still talking into it. "I'll call you back," she said hastily as she stood and hurried to meet the detectives on the sidewalk leading to the porch of her home.

"Why, it's Little Miss Silly-Tilley, all grown up," Bill O'Brien said from the porch where he still sat.

"Roxanne Tilley?" the short little Emma said as she looked up at the young woman. "Oh my heavens!" Emma blurted as she glanced at the badge and gun holster on the young woman's hip. "That's right; I heard you were going to the police academy but that was long ago. And I remember you always did want to be a Charlie's Angel when you were growing up." Emma took Tilley's hands in hers and looked her up and down as her face lit up with excitement before she looked over to Dodge. "We used to watch Charlie's Angels reruns together. Roxanne always wanted to know why there were no black Angels like her." Emma's eyes kept darting between Dodge and Tilley as she rambled on. "You know they got a Chinese Angel now. In the movies, you know. No black Angels, but a Chinese one. At least I think she's Chinese." Emma smiled before turning to Dodge again. "We watched reruns all the time."

Detective Tilley felt Emma's cold hands clutching hers as embarrassment washed over her while ignoring Dodge's muffled snickering from behind her.

"Would you like some tea and scones?" Bill asked loudly from where he still sat. "Emma, go put on some tea for our guests."

"They don't want tea, you idiot," Emma shouted, while her grip tightened on Tilley's hands. "They've already had frappuccinos from the coffee shop, remember!"

Dodge couldn't help but be reminded of Betty White, whom he adored, when he looked at Emma. Her curly white hair, glasses, and gentle smile helped mask a feistiness that was clearly apparent when she spoke.

"Is Charlie Dead?" Emma asked as she took on a very serious look. "My friend Myrtle was asking. She wants to be sure so she can post it on the Facebook, you know."

Dodge stepped closer to Tilley as he spoke. "We were wondering if you or your husband might have seen anything suspicious last night or this morning. Out of the ordinary, perhaps?"

"Oh, there was nothing ordinary about Charlie," Emma replied with a coy smile.

"Emma!" Bill shouted from the steps, cutting her off.

"Oh, shush up, Bill!" Emma shouted, brow furrowed, which quickly disappeared and was replaced with a wide smile. "Ms. Weatherbee came over wearing a big overcoat in this heat. It's too hot for a coat liked that. I bet she was naked underneath."

"Emma!" Bill shouted again.

"She didn't stay, though. Poor Ms. Weatherbee's probably sex-starved since her divorce."

"Emma!" Bill shouted.

"Like a cat in heat," Emma quipped. "And that Wilkins woman came by, too. She's that lawyer that teaches aerobics. Drives a white car."

Tilley knew Wilkins from the gym. She glanced at Dodge and saw he was taking notes and turned to Emma again who still had a hold of her hands. Emma's eyes were downcast now as she looked to be deep in thought.

"You should talk to Lucy Shaffer, too," added a pensive Emma. "She's a professional comedian, you know, from Hollywood."

"Was she here this morning?" Dodge asked. He knew exactly who Lucy Shaffer was. She had been seen in Poplar Falls and the gossip was that she was a guest of the Magnolia Wellness Centre.

"Oh no, but she was there last week or was that the week before," said a pensive Emma. "She was at the rehab centre. Booze, you know."

"Emma!" Bill said sternly.

"I'm just trying to be helpful," Emma said, smiling, before she took on a more serious look. "Is Charlie dead?"

"Yup," Bill shouted. "He's dead all right."

Dodge looked over at Bill and saw that he was peering across the street through his binoculars. Dodge turned and saw three men clumsily carrying a stretcher down the steps from the second-floor balcony. The body, in a body bag, was strapped to the stretcher.

"The ladies at my knitting group say Charlie had a big one," Emma stated with a smile. "A very big one." Emma shrugged and crumpled her nose in a cheeky fashion.

"Emma, for Christ's sake!" Bill shouted.

"That's all I can think of. But if you give me your card, like on TV, then I can call you if I think of anything else," Emma said with a smile as she looked Dodge up and down. She turned to Tilley and winked. "Handsome, isn't he."

Dodge handed Emma cards with both the detectives' information, making her finally let go of Detective Tilley's hands in the process. Emma smiled as she took the cards, looking them over with fascination.

"I hope I was helpful," Emma said as she again scanned Dodge and smiled.

"You were more than helpful, ma'am," Dodge replied.

"Thank you, Emma," Tilley added as she waved to Bill, who was too busy watching the goings-on across the street to even notice.

As the detectives made their way to the sidewalk, Dodge glanced back to make sure Emma couldn't hear him. He saw she had sat next to her husband on the porch.

"Is it just me or could you smell it, too?"

Tilley's reaction was enough to confirm that he had indeed smelled what he thought he'd smelled, and so there was no need to discuss that anymore.

"Charlie's Angels, huh?" he inquired.

"Shut up!" Tilley blurted.

Dodge glanced back to see Emma waving her hands about again, and this time he saw that she was spraying some sort of deodorant to mask the distinct odour as best as possible.

Bill set down his binoculars when he saw the detectives heading down the sidewalk and dug out a fancy Zippo lighter from his shirt pocket. Emma picked up the half-smoked joint from the wooden armrest between them; the same armrest that was marked with multiple burn marks. Bill took hold of the joint and gave his wife a glare of disapproval, knowing full well she would read into it what he was saying without having to vocalize any of it. He lit the joint, took a drag, and then handed it to Emma. He coughed twice before exhaling.

"You said too much," Bill told Emma.

"I did not," Emma replied. "I only told them half of it; less than half." Emma took a drag from the joint.

"They'll be back," Bill replied as he watched them walk toward the neighbour's house where a small red sports car had pulled into the drive.

"I had to say something," Emma replied as she scooped up her cordless phone and pushed redial. "Otherwise they'd know we where hiding something."

6

"This is like something out of a cheesy novel," Detective Tilley said as they walked up the driveway of the neighbour's house.

"You think we can believe the O'Brien's?" Dodge asked.

Detective Tilley gave no response as she gestured for Dodge to look at the older model red corvette, with the word RED on the vanity plate.

Dodge elbowed Tilley and pointed to the For Sale sign on the lawn of the home.

RED Realty Inc. Marci Grant.

The sign had a picture of a beautiful redhead with unbelievably white teeth next to a phone number. Dodge took a picture of the sign with his Blackberry just as the tall, leggy redhead stepped out of the car; high heels exiting first followed by a form-fitting skirt. Her business apparel hugged her body, showing off her figure. Her lipstick, eyeliner, long eyelashes, and outfit clashed with her beaten brown leather driving gloves which looked to be coming apart at the seams. Smiling, she peeled off one of the gloves before walking over with an extended bare hand.

"You must be the Blanchards," Marci Grant said with a smile. "I didn't know you were a cop," she added, clearly looking at the badge on Tilley's belt.

Tilley shook Marci Grant's hand as she spoke.

"I'm Detective Roxanne Tilley and this is my partner, Detective Franklin Dodge."

Marci looked across the street and then at the detectives. "Is that… is that Charlie Baker's place?" Marci inquired.

"Did you know Charlie?" Dodge asked as he took out a small notepad.

Marci's gaze lingered on the scene across the street as if she hadn't heard Dodge. She watched crime scene people come out of the upstairs apartment with containers and place them in a vehicle as the crowd observed. It didn't look quite as glamorous as they made it look on television, she thought.

"How long have you been sleeping with Charlie Baker?" Tilley asked bluntly, surprising Dodge in the process. Tilley watched Marci closely, trying to pick up on her body language in the process. "Miss Grant, how long?"

"Marci," the tall redhead replied. "Call me Marci." She turned her attention back to the detectives. Marci's eyes roamed all over Detective Tilley's body as she spoke with a smirk on her face. "Oh, I wasn't sleeping with Charlie. I was trying to sell him this house."

"I see," Tilley replied as she glanced at Dodge uncomfortably.

Dodge fought back a smile as he took notes.

Marci looked down at Tilley's breasts as she spoke again.

"Big dick or no big dick, Charlie's just not my type, honey."

"How long have you known Charlie?" Dodge asked.

Marci locked eyes with Dodge as she replied. "What? The O'Brien's didn't tell you that?"

"We'd rather hear it from you," Dodge replied.

"Charlie called me about four, maybe five weeks ago to ask about this house. I hinted a little, tried to tell him he should look at other houses with less nosy neighbours, but Charlie really liked this one."

"What time do you expect the owners to be home?" Dodge asked.

"The Turlingtons?" Marci replied. "They moved to Alberta almost four months ago. Took a job up there and hired me to sell their house."

"So the house has been vacant since?" Dodge asked as he jotted down more notes.

"Yes, Charlie actually called me last night to tell me he wanted to make an official offer on the house, but I already had a showing booked today with the Blanchards."

"Did he?" Dodge asked. "Make the offer?"

"He told me to come and see him this afternoon after I show it to the Blanchards." Marci's gaze went across the street again as she pointed a perfectly manicured fingernail in that direction. "Is...is he?"

"Dead," Detective Tilley replied as she watched Marci's body language for a reaction.

"Suicide?" Marci asked. "Can't be. People who are about to kill themselves don't make offers on houses."

"We're investigating," Dodge said as he shot Tilley a disapproving glance. She was volunteering too much information instead of letting her talk. It felt like a rookie move but Dodge knew she was usually better than this. It was obvious she wasn't comfortable, and it was affecting her judgement.

"Well, he obviously didn't die of natural causes or you wouldn't be asking questions," Marci replied with a grin. "Some guy probably caught him with his wife and shot him."

A large truck pulled into the driveway behind Marci's Corvette and killed its engine.

"*That* must be the Blanchards," Dodge said as he put

away his notepad and dug out a business card to give to Marci. "We may need to talk to you again."

Marci dug through her purse and quickly pulled out a pair of cards of her own. She handed one to Dodge and then smiled when she handed one to Tilley.

"Call me if you need anything," she said to Detective Tilley. "Call me...anytime."

Dodge grinned like a schoolboy as they walked away. Tilley ignored the moment of immaturity from her much older partner. Dodge didn't lose his composure very often, but today seemed to be an exception, thought Tilley as they walked away. She hoped it wasn't affecting his judgement.

7

Moments later, Marci Grant greeted her potential buyers with her usual big white smile and firm handshake. She turned to see the O'Briens still on their porch, watching things unfold. Marci saw a grinning Emma wave hello to her as she chatted on a cordless phone. Mr. Blanchard gestured towards the O'Brien residence as he spoke.

"You know the neighbours?"

"The O'Briens?" Marci asked. "A little bit. They're both retired I think," which was a half lie. With the Blanchards being from out of town, Marci figured she didn't need to tell them the full truth about the nosy old couple. "They're very friendly," Marci added with her trademark smile, flashing her abnormally white teeth.

"What's going on across the street?" Mrs. Blanchard asked with an expression of concern.

Before Marci could answer the question, a ringtone emanated from her purse, playing a familiar little song.

"Soft Kitty, Warm Kitty..."

Blushing slightly she dug her phone out of her purse,

answering quickly, cutting off the song made famous by the popular television sitcom. The only silly ringtone she had in her entire list of contacts. The one set for a specific caller. The name on the display read Trudy Wilkins. She flashed her index finger at the Blanchards with a weak smile, indicating she would just be a moment as she began walking away for a little privacy.

"Sorry, but I have to take this. It's my lawyer," Marci said as she answered the call. "Hey."

"Is this a bad time?" Trudy asked. She could tell it was from the way Marci answered, but she asked out of politeness.

"I'm with clients, yes. But never mind that; you were up awfully early this morning."

"I couldn't sleep," Trudy replied. "I figured I'd head to the gym and let you sleep."

"Aren't you the one and only early bird," Marci said in a knowing tone as she debated how much she should divulge. Should she confess as to how much she knew, she wondered.

"Hey, aren't you showing the Turlington house today?"

"Yes," Marci replied, as she thought it odd for Trudy to ask this. Trudy never really cared about the details of Marci's realtor business. Unless it was a closing she had to process paperwork for, she really didn't ever want to hear about her meeting strangers and showing houses. "Yes, I'm there now. Why do you ask?"

"Isn't that across the street from that apartment building?"

"There's an apartment building across the street. Yes, why?"

"I was just curious. I saw a post on Facebook about something going on there and was curious to know what it was," Trudy said. "Plus I saw a picture of you talking to a couple. I thought I'd ask. But I can tell it's a bad time, so we'll talk later. Sorry to bother you."

Before Marci could reply, Trudy had ended the call. Marci looked at her phone while she processed what had just happened. Trudy was a busy lawyer and was never on social media during the day. Maybe they needed to have a talk about certain issues after all. But that would have to wait. She shot a glance across the street at the crowd of people watching things unfold as she refocused her attention to the matter at hand, which was doing what the Turlingtons had hired her to do. Sell their house.

"I'm so sorry, but I needed to take that," Marci stated as she put the phone in her purse and joined the Blanchards on the sidewalk, to what would eventually become their new home. "My clients are very important and some calls can't be ignored." Marci was lying, but as usual nobody could tell. She was good at it.

8

Meanwhile, Emma was still on the porch and back on the phone with her friend Myrtle, filling her in on the goings-on at their friend Agatha's apartment building across the street. And also, how that redheaded, lesbian, real-estate slut Marci Grant was showing the neighbours' house again. Slut was what Emma called Marci behind her back. Emma usually liked everyone, unless they didn't like her, and she knew full well Marci Grant wasn't a fan of hers.

"I miss the Turlingtons. I mean, they were weird and all but at least they were sorta normal," Emma said. "I just hope these people aren't serial killers. Or worse, religious nuts," Emma said to her friend.

Myrtle laughed at Emma's comment before getting to the point she wanted to make. "I'm thinking we should have an emergency meeting tonight."

"Tonight?" Emma asked. "Bill and I had plans." Emma

shot a glance at Bill, who was enthralled behind his huge pair of binoculars.

"Cancel," Myrtle blurted. "With everything that's going on across the street, we need to call an emergency meeting."

"Okay," Emma replied. "Bill won't like that I'm cancelling our night."

Bill lowered the binoculars and gave Emma a dirty look. He was listening after all, she thought.

"Oh shush, if you know what's good for you," Emma said to Bill. "Not you, Myrtle. Bill just gave me the stink eye."

"I'll call Ester and Mavis. You call Geraldine and Agatha."

"Okay," Emma replied. "But Agatha's at the police station being questioned. She's probably a suspect or something."

"Oh my," Myrtle replied. "Oh my goodness!"

Both women laughed.

"Isn't this exciting?" Myrtle asked.

9

Later that night, under a blanket of stars, Detective Tilley pulled her car into her driveway and killed the engine. She sat still for a moment, adjusting her rear view mirror. From across the street she could see a familiar glow coming from the otherwise dark screened-in porch at her partner's house. When the faint light flickered she took this to mean that Dodge was still awake, which wasn't a surprise as he had been doing this ever since their last case went cold. Getting out of her car, she walked across the street. Dodge lit a small lamp as she approached.

"Good workout?" he asked as a yoga pants and hoodie-clad Tilley climbed the steps to his porch. From the little Dodge could see in the dark, her hair was matted as it usually was after a serious visit to the gym.

"Yup, the usual," Tilley replied. What she didn't confess

was the need to burn off the nervous energy a new case of this magnitude stirred up. How, if she didn't burn off some steam, she wouldn't sleep a wink. "How was your run?"

"Good," he replied, sitting in the dark still in his running shorts, damp with perspiration, while he nursed a cold beer. He ran almost every night but doubled his run when he had something on his mind. He hadn't forgotten not being able to catch the perp stealing women's underwear. The one the local press named the Panty Bandit. The thought of him still being out there bothered Dodge, and it was obvious to most everyone who knew him. Dodge fiddled with the old Dell laptop computer which sat in his lap.

"Beer?" he asked, gesturing to an old cabinet near the door of the porch.

Tilley opened the cabinet door to reveal a hidden mini fridge containing both full and empty beer cans. She took a beer and perched herself on the cabinet fridge.

"Remind me again," Tilley asked, "why you started keeping your empty beer cans in the fridge?"

"It's too warm in here," he said referring to the screened porch he always drank beer in on warm summer nights. "No fruit flies that way."

"You're one strange cat," Tilley said. She pointed to a pile of newspapers on the floor. "Anything in those?"

"The local press headlined the murder but talk in circles since they really know nothing."

"So what are you up to now, other than looking creepy sitting here in the dark?"

"Surfing Facebook," Dodge replied. "Checking out all the pictures and videos people posted from outside Charlie Baker's place."

"Good idea," Tilley replied as she sipped the beer and got closer to see the laptop's screen, which had caused the strange glow in the otherwise-dark screened porch. "Find anything good?"

"Sorta," Dodge replied. "Check this out."

A few moments later they were watching a video clip which scanned the crowd standing by the yellow police tape. The video was a mere 32 seconds long.

"Who's she?" Tilley asked before sipping more beer.

"Exactly," Dodge said. "That's what I want to know."

"Walter seems to know her," Tilley said. She was referring to a young, simple-looking, thin man in baggy clothes and crooked baseball cap. He stood next to his adult-sized tricycle which was complete with two wire baskets (front and back). Hooked to the back was a small trailer cart near full of empty bottles and cans. Standing next to Walter was a tiny brunette, mid-30s, who looked to be sobbing hard. Tears ran down her face as she clutched a large purse to her bosom.

"She seems way too upset to *not* have known Charlie," Dodge replied.

"A year ago, you could have asked Walter who she is," Tilley stated incorrectly. It was more than a year. A little over eighteen months, to be more precise.

"I know," Dodge replied. Walter hadn't been this way in his youth. He wasn't a genius, but he was as smart as most other kids his age. But since the doctors took out a brain tumour and he suffered a brain haemorrhage, his entire vocabulary now consisted of little more than the days of the week.

Tilley finished her beer and showed the empty can to Dodge as if to ask where to put it.

"Just leave it there," he said, gesturing to the top of the cabinet. "I need to put them out for Walter anyway. I'm Wednesday."

"Well, show that to the guys at the station tomorrow. She's cute enough that someone in the office is bound to know who she is." Tilley set the can down on the cabinet. "Goodnight!" she said as she exited the porch and headed home.

Dodge closed his fake Facebook account and shut down his laptop. He went to the kitchen and came back with a blue transparent trash bag, collecting the empties from his fridge and anywhere else they might be while his mind wandered to Walter. If Walter wasn't a simple-minded fool with brain damage, he might have been more confident in his ability to read lips, thought Dodge. He wasn't sure, but what he assumed Walter was saying to the brunette was 'Tuesday' and if Dodge was right that meant she was from Poplar Falls. If he was right, that would mean she would live not that far away and was a regular of Walter's. Walter would collect her recyclables on Tuesdays, which would narrow down the area she lived in. He didn't know Walter's route well, but he knew enough to know this. Dodge mulled this over as he took the bag outside. He finished his beer and placed the empty can in the bag, then tied it shut and placed the bag of cans next to a second bag containing more empty beer cans and juice containers near his porch steps. Walter would pick them up the next morning, as Dodge was Wednesday after all.

10

At the age of 31, Chadwick Lemkie had taken the job of lead Crime Scene Investigator in Poplar Falls to further his career. In any major metropolis, such leadership positions were reserved for more experienced senior crime scene investigators. The ones with a lot more field experience and better qualified to lead. But the police chief had wanted someone independent who was both lab- and field-proficient and using the title of lead CSI worked like a charm. He attracted many interested applicants. 'Lead CSI' was just a title since this person would be the entire department. Poplar Falls wasn't exactly crime central. Mostly thefts and assaults, murders were incredibly rare. Sure there were the occasional suspicious deaths, but most of the time those could be explained; almost always quickly determined as accidental or of natural causes right at the scene. Lemkie had been excited to get the position, even if he had still been doing the same work as before and had nobody to lead, he didn't care, and he proved himself early on as a great investigator.

Lemkie had managed well on his own for nearly five years until the Panty Bandit. His usual case load was not a problem, but when the new case added dozens of homes to investigate Lemkie suddenly found himself overwhelmed. Sending stuff out of town to be processed wasn't an option the chief could allow, under the circumstances. The mayor was on his back about the local press and he didn't want that spreading. But with so many peculiar burglaries in a short period of time, the townsfolk feared for their safety. In an effort to get this case resolved quickly, the chief had agreed to let Lemkie hire Calvin on a six-month contract. He proved very knowledgeable for someone fresh out of school and eager to prove himself. Then suddenly one day, the mysterious thefts stopped just as suddenly as they had begun. The last burglary was just like the rest and so they had assumed there would be others. But after three months, Lemkie predicted there would be no more and he was right. But after the six months were up Calvin was kept on.

Now faced with their very first real murder since coming to Poplar Falls, Lemkie and Calvin would take no chances. They had photographed every inch of Charlie's apartment, even the most mundane items that probably had nothing to do with Charlie's death. They had also bagged and tagged a ridiculous amount of stuff from the apartment and now were cataloguing it all. It was hard to tell what might end up being the thing that would solve the crime, so they took practically everything. They had spent hours collecting so many fingerprints that Lemkie didn't think they would be of much help. But they had taken them anyway to be thorough. They had bobby pins, scrunchies, and multiple hair ties all with different color hair stuck in them. Fourteen buttons of various sizes and color with threads still stuck to them were found under the furniture. Lemkie commented that perhaps clothing had often been removed in a hurry at Charlie's place. They found a pair of pink patent leather pumps under the bed, too small to be something Charlie wore, Calvin had said jokingly. They had laid out and catalogued the contents of trash cans and other garbage that had littered Charlie's apartment. The trash can contained a large collection of empty lube containers, used condoms, feminine hygiene products, and a small broken remote covered in something sticky.

On a separate table in the lab sat all the devices that had hidden cameras in them. They found a plastic rabbit with a camera for an eye; a hollowed-out book with a lens in its spine; a reading lamp above the bed with a lens for a button, and an old VCR with not only a lens but a portable hard drive inside it as well. This recent discovery had the pair of CSIs hatching plans on how to handle the workload. Calvin was good with computers, and so he would be the one to see what was on the electronic device. This he offered to do gladly, though he would come to regret the decision. At the time, hacking into the hard drive was way more appealing than collecting DNA from used condoms and lube containers.

11

The following morning both detectives sat at their desks, quietly sipping coffee and going over photos of the evidence that had been catalogued so far. This peculiar case is one for the books, Dodge kept telling everyone. Strewn on his desk were printed copies of the same images Tilley was viewing on the screen of her laptop.

"So, I started a list of women I think Charlie was sleeping with," Dodge said with a sly, immature grin. "I added Marci Grant to that list but took her off again since I figure you'd be more her type than Charlie."

"You think?" Tilley replied with an air of sarcasm as she stuck a pen in her mouth, clicking through the pictures on her computer.

"You think he was sleeping with Ms. Weatherbee?" He leaned back in his chair with coffee in hand and put his feet up.

Tilley grinned, chewing on her pen a bit before spitting it out to reply.

"To be honest, I don't know. She looked nervous. I've known her since I was in the fifth grade; Ms. Weatherbee is not the nervous type. So for her to be nervous I can only assume they weren't lovers, and that this was probably the first time she was over at his place."

"Maybe," Dodge replied. "I think we should talk to her anyway."

"Sure," Tilley replied. "She might know something."

Dodge settled down in front of his old laptop again and logged into Facebook using his fake account. He quickly found what he was looking for and saved a picture of the sobbing brunette from the crime scene. It was a better one than the picture he had saved the previous evening.

"I'm assuming we're going to have a long list of suspects, but this one intrigues me," he said as he sent a copy of the woman's picture to the office printer.

"But we really only need one suspect," Tilley replied with a smirk. "The guilty one."

Dodge chuckled. This, if anything, was Tilley's mantra, which he poked fun at as often as he could while trying not to make her mad.

Tilley scanned through the evidence photos, pausing at one in particular which showed multiple objects on a table: a pink hairbrush full of long blonde hairs, a black elastic band which looked to have the same hair color clung to it, a tube of lip balm, a brown button with a few coins, and a few small identical white buttons. The blonde hairs intrigued her, but she couldn't see any other color hairs in the brush. The next image was of a VCR that had been opened and inside was a small, modern-looking black box.

"Is that what I think it is?" Tilley said aloud.

"Probably," she heard someone say before looking to see who it was. Lead CSI Lemkie walked over to Dodge and handed him a page from the printer. "It's a cleverly hidden portable hard drive, is what that is."

"Really," Tilley replied. "What's on it?"

"We don't know yet. It's password-protected but Calvin's working on hacking it."

"What about those wires that looked to have led to something that was taken?" Tilley asked.

"We're pretty sure that was a laptop," Lemkie replied before he turned to Dodge. "Why do you have a picture of Sadie?"

"Who?" Dodge asked.

"Her." Lemkie pointed to the printed picture he had just given Dodge. "Sadie."

"You know her?" Tilley asked, spinning her chair completely away from her desk and dedicating her full attention to the conversation at hand.

"That's Sadie Cross," Lemkie replied. "She owns the daycare my son goes to."

"Which one?" Dodge asked, digging though the papers on his desk for a pen.

"Sunshine and Rainbows," Lemkie said as he proceeded to give them the address. "But you still haven't told me why you have her picture. Don't tell me you think she knew Charlie Baker?"

"That's what I want to know," Dodge stated as he examined the picture.

"Her husband runs a butcher shop downtown," Lemkie stated matter-of-factly, as if that would prove she couldn't possibly know Charlie Baker. "Vernon's Meats," he added. "Very friendly fellow; makes his own meat pies, which are amazing by the way."

"I know him," Tilley said. "Well, sorta. I buy all my meat at his shop. I didn't know he had a wife."

"Interesting," Dodge stated as he took notes. "Two new suspects just like that."

"Two?" Lemkie asked. "Sadie is one of the sweetest women I know."

"Appearances can be deceiving," Tilley said.

"Trust me," Lemkie said.

"I do," Dodge said. "But she's definitely going on the list."

"You'll see what I mean when you meet her," Lemkie replied. "That woman couldn't hurt a fly if she tried."

12

Later that afternoon the detectives found themselves in a room that smelled of poo as they were knee-deep in kids, which included quite a few toddlers. Soft-spoken Sadie and her staff obviously had their hands full as little Thomas, Lemkie's son, had been belted in the face with a toy truck by an upset little girl in pigtails. Obviously a dispute over possession of the toy truck noted Dodge, as he and Tilley were ushered into an office in the back by one of the other caregivers.

Tilley looked over the pictures hung on the office walls. Most were of Sadie with children of all ages, but there were a few of her with a burly-looking man who she knew was Vernon, Sadie's husband. Meanwhile, Dodge watched the commotion through the office window as Sadie coddled little Thomas, calming him down before passing him off to another of the caregivers. Sadie came across as mild-mannered even when she scolded the young girl in the pigtails. She smiled at little Thomas before handing over the reins to the other women, while she met in private with the detectives.

Entering the office, Sadie gestured for the detectives to sit in chairs normally for the parents of her kids. A curious little girl pressed her face against the glass of the large office window that overlooked the daycare, watching Sadie and the detectives. Sadie smiled and waved to the little girl as she closed the blind before sitting at her desk.

"What can I help you with?" Sadie Cross inquired while smiling.

"We were wondering how you knew Charlie Baker," Dodge stated.

"Who?" asked Sadie, her smile vanishing.

"Charlie Baker." Dodge laid a picture of a clearly upset Sadie on the desk. In the picture, Sadie was standing behind the yellow police tape.

"Yeah, I was fucking him," Sadie replied in a surprisingly blunt tone of voice, which caught Dodge by surprise, while Tilley's expression didn't change. She was no longer the demure, soft-spoken woman they had met when they arrived.

"But can you blame me?" Sadie blurted as she opened a desk drawer and pulled out a giant, half-eaten chocolate bar. She peeled back the foil and took a large bite of what looked and smelled like dark chocolate. Her face flushed, she chewed while she turned her attention to the pictures on her wall. "Sunshine and fucking Rainbows, my ass!" she stated as she chewed. "It's all over town, and all over fucking Facebook, that I was screwing Charlie." Sadie took a smaller bite of chocolate this time as she continued what was becoming a rant. "You should see the way the fathers look at me now. And the mothers... holy cats! The judgemental looks I get from most of them. A few of them are jealous and pissed that it was me and not them. GOD!"

"Does your husband know?" Dodge asked calmly as he

took notes.

"Probably," Sadie replied as she took another small bite of chocolate before offering some to Tilley, who gently refused. "It's dark chocolate. It's good for you." Sadie smiled weakly before wrapping the rest of the chocolate in the foil and putting it back in the drawer.

"Vernon hasn't made love to me in four years. FOUR YEARS!" Sadie said loudly. "Being married to Vernon is like always being hungry for steak but not being able to eat it. So I had a fucking hamburger instead. A BIG fat juicy one at that!"

"Where were you the morning of..." Dodge started before Sadie cut him off.

"I sure as HELL didn't kill Charlie, if that's what you're implying. Hell NO, best lay I ever had, and I for one am gonna miss that huge dick of his."

"Could your husband have maybe..."

"Vernon?" Sadie blurted with a sharp laugh. "Vernon was jealous all right, but not because another man was fucking his wife. Hell NO! He'd heard rumours of how big Charlie was. How good he was. Vernon probably wanted to fuck Charlie himself. Hell, I wish he'd just fucking come out already. GOD! It would make leaving him so much easier."

Tilley shot a glance at Dodge, giving him a look that he knew well. That look meant, 'Let's wrap this up and get out of here'. And Dodge, feeling satisfied with what he had heard so far, decided this might be a good idea. They would most likely talk to Sadie again, but best to come back later. Let her stew on the conversation for a bit and calm down some.

Dodge dug out a business card and extended it towards Sadie as he spoke. "Well, thank you for taking the time to talk to us," he stated.

"Vernon doesn't only make sausages—he loves them, too, you know. I bet that bitch Emma knows who killed my Charlie." A tear ran down Sadie's cheek as she wiped it away quickly. "Fucking, nosy Emma O'Brien and her gossipy old crows." Sadie took out her chocolate, took a bite, and put it away again.

"Are we done here?" she asked while she chewed. "I've gotta get back to the kids before those little lovable booger-snots eat my staff alive."

As the detectives were leaving, Dodge couldn't help but marvel at the amazing transformation of the woman named Sadie Cross. Now she was the demure little woman again, smiling and laughing with the children—their happy little faces glowing at the sound of the daycare owner's laughter. All was well again between Thomas and the little girl in the pigtails. The toy truck was gone now and they were playing on a giant plastic kitchenette. Thomas still had a large red mark from the toy truck on his face, but he didn't seem to care as he helped his little friend take something from the fake oven.

13

"I was looking at Charlie's financial records," Tilley stated as she sat at her desk working on her computer. "I think I know what brought Charlie Baker to Poplar Falls."

"Do tell," Dodge replied as he sat at his own desk with a fresh cup of coffee.

"Two days after he moved here, he paid a pretty hefty sum to the Magnolia Wellness and Rehabilitation Centre."

"Interesting," Dodge replied.

"I'll say," Tilley replied. "It actually explains why he had an apartment in town, too. I mean, living on the grounds is very expensive. So taking a small apartment in town would be a better idea."

"True," Dodge replied. "Plus, he'd have more privacy, too, considering his lifestyle choices."

"Odd part is the payments stopped about three months ago."

"Well maybe he was cured? No?"

"He wasn't there for drugs or alcohol," Tilley said as she paused and checked her own coffee cup. "If he was we'd have found something. The place was clean of that. I mean, a couple of bottles of wine don't constitute alcoholism."

"Meaning?" Dodge asked.

"Meaning he had to be there for sexual addiction," Tilley replied. "That's what I'm betting on."

"Yeah, well, that's a bit obvious, considering the circumstances," Dodge replied.

"True," Tilley replied as she proceeded to get herself more coffee.

Soon after they discovered a large refund of money from the Wellness Centre, and the detectives spent the next half hour discussing possible reasons for such a credit and planned to inquire about it. Tilley mentioned a visit to the owners of the Wellness Centre, as she knew them well. Dodge never thought to inquire who they were, but would know soon enough.

14

"You wanted to see us," Dodge said as he and Tilley entered Lemkie's lab.

"Ah, yes," Lemkie replied as he got up from his computer and dug out three different evidence bags from a white storage box and placed them on a table between himself and the detectives. Each sealed evidence bag contained a prescription pill bottle, each with a different label. One bottle was empty, another had a small number of blue pills, while the other contained a little over half a bottle.

"Viagra?" Dodge asked.

"Of course," Lemkie replied. "But that's not the interesting part."

Tilley picked up the first bag with the empty bottle and turned it over to read the barely legible moisture-damaged label.

"Who's Albert Johnson?" Tilley asked as she set the bagged pill bottle down and picked up another.

"From everything I've found so far, I assume he was a client of the Rehab Clinic," Lemkie replied.

"He's from Stonevalley," Dodge said. Lemkie and Tilley met this statement with puzzled looks. "I met him about a month ago," Dodge added. "I gave him a warning and sent him on his way."

"For?" Tilley inquired.

"Public nudity," Dodge replied. "I was at Alice's Dairy Spot out on Hazelnut Drive and some lady told me she had seen some guy, half-naked, just up the road from the dairy bar. Looked like he was playing with himself or something, so I checked it out. Too many kids around, you know. Anyway, he said he just stopped to have a piss. Couldn't wait to find a bathroom."

"You let him go?" Lemkie asked.

"The story sounded legit and I had no other way to prove it. Besides, he was heading out of town and I called in a favour to check him out."

Tilley looked at the second bottle and smiled, but when she showed it to Dodge her smile quickly faded.

"Bill O'Brien? Emma's Bill?"

"Yup," Tilley replied. "That's his address on the bottle."

"And the third is a Simon Doiron. But the address doesn't exist and so I have a feeling Simon doesn't either," added Lemkie. "And that's all fine and dandy, but that's not what I found interesting in the least bit. What I found fascinating was the prints on two of the bottles."

"Two?" Tilley asked.

"I assume the prints on the O'Brien bottle were Bill's and, of course, Charlie's prints were on it, too. Still waiting on some searches on those, but I found these on the other two bottles," Lemkie stated as he handed Tilley a beige folder.

"Stella Rubbin," Lemkie said as Tilley opened the folder to reveal a police mug shot of a dishevelled Stella. "She has an interesting record of petty stuff, but it's a long list. Drunk and disorderly, driving under the influence, assault, assaulting a police officer, and the list goes on. She even did a little time."

"I've seen her in town before," Tilley said. Stella, a busty black woman in a town full of mostly white people, stood out to Tilley. "I'm sure of it."

"From what I can see," Lemkie replied as he reached over and flipped a page in the folder. "She used to be a manager at a posh hotel in California before she went to prison. Now she's the manager at the Wellness Centre." Lemkie pulled out a pamphlet from the back of the folder and plopped it on top of the page Tilley was looking at. At the bottom of the back page of the pamphlet was Stella Rubbin's name with the title of manager, confirming what Lemkie said.

"What would her prints be doing on those pill bottles?" Tilley asked.

"If the clinic treats people for sexual addiction like you said," Dodge replied. "Then perhaps Charlie Baker took the pills from the clinic. She might have been holding on to them or something; or maybe confiscated them in the case of Johnson, for example. Can I get a copy of this folder?" Dodge asked.

"That's your copy," Lemkie replied with a smirk. "I printed it for you. Tilley can get a copy from the shared folder in Q drive like everyone else does."

Dodge ignored the sarcasm about his love of the printed page and the fancy computer lingo, taking the folder from

Tilley. He leafed through it briefly as he turned to leave and paused at the doorway, waiting for his partner.

"Where are you with the hard drive?" Tilley inquired.

"Oh, that reminds me," Lemkie said as he took a plastic shopping bag from his desk and smiled. "I'm going to go find that out right now."

"What's in the bag?" Dodge asked.

"This?" Lemkie said in a light-hearted tone as he held the bag before him. "Nothing much; just some lotion and a box of tissues for Calvin. He's been watching Charlie Baker's porn for close to two days now, so I got him this."

The two of them laughed all the way down the hallway and back to their desks while Lemkie delivered his goods to Calvin, who sheepishly smiled and then used a flurry of curse words that would have made his late mother blush twenty shades of red.

15

After a quick meal, Tilley had gone to the office that evening with the intention of sorting through the case file she had on the Charlie Baker murder. She hoped that organizing her notes and reviewing everything might help her make sense of it all. She opened her email and found a message from Calvin. The email was addressed to Lemkie, Dodge, and herself, and was brief. Calvin explained that without the proper software, which he had asked for but they didn't have the budget to get, he had tried to collect good pictures of all the faces from the hard drive. The email also contained a link to the Q drive where Calvin had compiled a folder of pictures of all the women in the home movies found on the hard drive. The folder contained fourteen faces, most nameless at this point, except a select few.

Tilley recognized Sadie Cross from the picture of her

smiling with downcast eyes. There was no doubt this woman was the demur little Sadie who owned Sunshine and Rainbows Daycare. Only she didn't quite appear as the mousy type in this picture. The woman's coy smile said all she needed to know about her relationship to Charlie Baker.

Another picture was of the famous comedian Lucy Shaffer. Tilley briefly wondered what a tabloid would pay for such a photo, but quickly dismissed the idea as stupid. (She would reflect on this again later that night. And she would speculate if Calvin, or perhaps Lemkie, had been on the same train of thought.)

Still sitting at her desk, and a few clicks of the mouse later, and she was looking at a picture of Stella Rubbin. The detectives had planned on a visit to the Magnolia Wellness Centre to talk to Stella, and this picture cemented the need. But first they would visit the owners of the clinic, as they had questions about Charlie Baker.

From amongst the pictures of women Tilley recognized the pretty blonde, Trudy Wilkins. Trudy was a prominent lawyer in town and apparently a lover of Charlie's as well. The rumours about Trudy must have been wrong, thought Tilley, although her instincts were usually never wrong about these things.

Tilley kept scrolling through the images, noting the ones she knew, the ones she thought looked familiar and, lastly, the ones that were a mystery to her. In her third scroll through, she realized that she had not seen her former teacher among the pictures. Her suspicions about Ms. Weatherbee never having been with Charlie might not be so far off, she thought. Then she wondered if this would make Dodge happy or sad. She couldn't help but notice how he paid extra attention whenever her name came up in conversation. They would have to visit her soon just in case, though. Tilley couldn't not, as it might look like she was playing favourites if people found out. And people would find out since Emma and Bill knew Ms. Weatherbee had been to Charlie's apartment the very morning he was found stiff as a board.

Tilley grabbed a Post-it pad and made a list of people to talk to. She would discuss this with Dodge in the morning over coffee and they would hatch a plan. Or maybe she wouldn't, thinking about the look on his face if she just showed him instead. That's when the idea struck her as too good to pass up and she smiled. Suddenly she couldn't wait until morning. And since Tilley still had steam to burn, a visit to the gym sounded just right.

16

As Dodge's rusty Ford Escape pulled up behind Tilley's car, he couldn't help but wonder why she had asked him to meet her at the O'Briens' house at this hour. It was almost seven in the morning and what he wanted to do was get to the station, grab coffee, and have a look at Charlie Baker's lady friends in the folder Tilley had told him about. Earlier that morning she had called him and had filled him in about the folder and how they had a full day ahead of them. She had insisted on getting started early and asked that he meet her at the O'Briens' house first.

The first thing Tilley did when Dodge arrived was to hand him a file folder, which she explained had copies of Charlie Baker's financial transactions. She had printed off the records that showed he had paid for therapy at the rehab centre. Dodge filled Tilley in on the gossip from Facebook he had found the night before. Charlie had been getting therapy at the Magnolia Rehab Centre, but people were talking about how he had gotten kicked out of the place. The last straw apparently had been when Charlie was caught having sex in a closet, and on more than a few occasions one lady had said. But these were just rumours of course, and worth looking into when they met Stella. But that would come later. Dodge put the paperwork in his car as he spoke. "Why couldn't this wait until later?"

"They won't be home later," Tilley replied. "And I wanted to catch them without anyone else to overhear."

"Elaborate, please," Dodge asked.

"There are things those financial records don't tell you," Tilley replied. "Remember late yesterday, when you called the clinic to speak to the manager, Stella Rubbin? Remember how that kid told you the manager wasn't available right now? He thought the owners were filling in for the manager or something?"

"Wait," Dodge replied. "Are you saying what I think you're saying?"

"The O'Briens' own the rehab centre," Tilley replied, who had to bite the inside of her mouth to prevent from smiling as she watched his reaction.

"Seriously?" Dodge asked. "I had heard some rich lady owned the place when I first moved to Poplar Falls."

"That would be Emma," Tilley replied as she walked up the steps of the porch of the O'Briens' home, Dodge right behind her. Tilley rang the doorbell and then heard someone shuffling about coming from inside the house.

"Coming," Emma shouted.

"Who could that be at this hour?" Bill said in his usual too loud voice, which sounded like he wanted the early birds to hear him.

Moments later Emma opened the door, wearing a fuzzy pink housecoat and matching slippers, her makeup and hair immaculate even if she wasn't dressed.

"You're here about the pills, aren't you?" Emma questioned before either of the detectives could even utter a greeting.

"Emma!" Bill shouted from somewhere out of sight.

"Oh, shush," Emma replied, half-hiding behind her front

door. "Be quiet if you know what's good for you."

"Promises, promises!" Bill replied.

"Yes," Tilley replied. "But we also wanted to talk about the payments for treatment at the rehab centre."

"That and we were wondering if the rumours are true that he was kicked out of the rehab clinic." Dodge amended.

"The money was for treatment at the clinic, for sexual addiction," Emma replied as she cast her gaze down as if she was thinking. They had seen her do this before and so they waited a moment, knowing full well she would soon volunteer more information than they had asked for.

"Some was for Viagra, too."

"Emma!" Bill shouted.

"That's it," Emma screamed. "You're in for it now!"

Tilley would later swear she heard Bill giggle a little when Emma said that.

"Viagra?" Dodge asked. "Wasn't he at the clinic because of a sex addiction?"

Dodge wondered briefly why you would supply a sex addict with pills like Viagra. The idea seemed counterproductive to any therapy the clinic was administering. But Emma always seemed more than happy to tell them everything, so he didn't have to wonder long. It was as if she loved the idea of being the one who knew the truth, and being able to tell them. And since Charlie Baker was dead, there wasn't any harm in telling the detectives.

"Yes, Viagra," Emma replied. "He would have bought them on the interweb or from some guy in an alley otherwise. People often use fake names to get it from sketchy pharmacists. And that's not always safe."

Tilley remembered the pill bottle labelled Simon Doiron with the fake address, and assumed that was what those were.

"True but doesn't that go against what you're doing at the rehab centre?" Dodge asked. He was curious now and wanted Emma's version.

"Well, we don't try and stop people from having sex," Emma replied with a large smile. "No, no. It's not like booze or drugs, you know. Those you have to quit. You can't just have a little. But not sex. Don't be silly. We try and teach them how to not let sex rule their lives."

Dodge marvelled at this answer as it was not what he had expected from the mature woman standing before him.

"Is it true that you asked him to leave the Centre?" Tilley asked.

"Yes, but only because he was keeping us from helping the others," Emma replied. "Lord knows we tried to help poor Charlie. We don't try and teach abstinence, we teach control. And Charlie was out of control."

"It didn't work with that damned Charlie Baker," Bill shouted, who was still out of sight.

Emma provided some rough dates that confirmed most of what the detectives already knew; mostly about the purchasing of the Viagra. They were soon satisfied with what they had been told, as Emma seemed sincere enough. But Dodge couldn't help but wonder why Emma had not volunteered this information sooner. She must have known they would find this out quickly enough. Perhaps she was embarrassed about this since she knew Tilley personally. He remembered Emma telling him about Tilley, the Charlie's Angel, and this suddenly struck Dodge as quite funny. He was able to stifle a laugh, but not the grin which suddenly appeared before he could stop it. He turned away from the ladies as he spoke his half-choked farewell, which he would then be required to explain to Tilley afterwards.

"Okay, we'll be in touch if we have any more questions," Tilley said as she walked off the stoop and down to the walkway following Dodge.

"Sorry we disturbed you," Dodge added, who had regained his composure.

"It's no trouble," Emma said with a smile.

Tilley heard Bill speaking loudly as she walked away.

"Are they gone yet?" Bill shouted.

"Shut your trap if you know what's good for you," Emma shouted as she shut the door.

When Dodge was over his sudden bout of chuckles and had reminisced about the Charlie's Angel joke, he asked Tilley if the O'Briens had a dog. To which Tilley replied that this was highly doubtful, as Emma was severely allergic to all types of fur. A fact that Dodge would say was strange since there was a dog dish on the floor in the hallway and a leash on the entryway table. Neither of them would voice their opinions on this but both were thinking the same thing. There was a reason the Wellness Clinic treated sex addicts, and they both knew it.

17

As Detectives Franklin Dodge and Roxanne Tilley slowly drove through the entry gates of the isolated Magnolia Wellness and Rehabilitation Centre, they marvelled at the ornate landscape. The abundance of magnolia trees, most of which were in bloom with beautiful pink flowers, were simply breathtaking. The perfectly manicured bushes and flowerbeds made Dodge wonder just how much work it took to maintain such a display. Meanwhile Tilley had other things on her mind.

"Really?" a miffed Tilley asked.

"What?" Dodge replied. "I didn't know that was back there. Probably fell out of a box while I was..."

"You didn't know you had women's underwear in the back of your car?"

"It was evidence," Dodge stated, choosing to leave out the part about sneaking Panty Bandit evidence boxes and files home on a few occasions.

"Oh, I know," Tilley replied, having suspected Dodge's obsession with the cold case was worse she thought. She hadn't known just how severe it was until now. "Thank God it was tagged and in an evidence bag."

Dodge smiled sheepishly as he spoke. "I didn't think he was going to search the vehicle that thoroughly."

"I bet they search the vehicle, he says," Tilley quipped. "Even though we're cops, they're still going to search it," she added while doing her best impression of her partner.

"I figured they would," Dodge replied. "They have to. Otherwise people would sneak in booze and drugs."

"Good thing you didn't have booze or drugs, too, then," Tilley replied, suspecting the security guard would end up having friends on the police force. Her worst fear was that this would get back to them and then the jokes and pranks would start.

To change the subject, Dodge pointed out a dark-haired women sitting on a park bench near a water fountain. She was dressed in a white housecoat, while sobbing into a fist-full of tissues while another woman in pyjamas tried to console her.

"Lifestyles of the rich and famous," Dodge said, referring to the rumoured famous guests who frequented the rehab centre.

As they pulled up to the main building, Tilley recalled coming to the centre in her youth. It was long ago, and she didn't remember it looking as extravagant then. Soon after the detectives were at the front desk, marvelling at Stephanie who was clearly not having a very good day so far.

"Look, if you're here about that big-titted, blonde bitch, she's not here, okay!" Stephanie blurted, wiping at a purple stain on the front off her uniform. She puffed at strands of hair that dangled in her face as she focused on getting the smoothie off her chest.

"Let me start over," Dodge said. "I'm Detective Franklin Dodge and this is my partner, Detective Roxanne Tilley. We'd like to speak to the manager if she's available."

"Look, I'm sorry, okay? I didn't mean to be rude, but," Stephanie said as she paused and pointed at the giant purple stain on her uniform, "I'm not exactly having the greatest day. So cut me some f'ing slack."

"We're here to see the manager..." Tilley started before being cut off.

"Damn it!" Stephanie marched off into a back room while another young woman in a dark burgundy uniform with a gold nametag exited from the same back room.

"I'm sorry about that," she said with an air of sincerity. "She's new and not used to dealing with recovering addicts," she added. "I'm Amber. Can I help you?"

"I'm Detective Franklin Dodge and this is Detective Roxanne Tilley. We're here to speak to the manager."

"Not about Stephanie," Tilley added. "It's about a case we're working on."

"Oh, I'm sorry, but the manager isn't available right now," Amber said. She glanced about to make sure no one was listening. "She fell off the wagon," she added in a hushed voice.

"I'm sorry?" Dodge assumed he had misunderstood.

"She was having a fling with one of our guests who died. At least that's what Stephanie's cousin Jeremy told her, that his friend Josh told him. Or was it her cousin Josh, who told Jeremy, who told her? Anyway, when Stella heard Charlie had died, she took to drinking again and hasn't exactly stopped since." Amber looked about again as if expecting to see someone eavesdropping. "She's an alcoholic," she whispered.

Dodge opened his mouth to speak but Amber cut him off.

"She was sober five years," she added. "That's what Josh told Jeremy, who told Stephanie. Or was it Jeremy who told Josh? Anyway... they found her wearing nothing but her underwear, drunk and swimming in one of the ponds on the centre grounds."

Dodge now had a notebook out and was jotting down notes. Tilley marvelled at how forthcoming Amber was with all this information without even knowing why they were there.

"Josh told Jeremy that Stella was trading pills for sex."

"Pills?" Tilley asked.

"Pills," Amber replied. "Viagra." She said this in a hushed voice, as if that was a dirty word. "She checked herself in after they found her in the pond."

"You want to see the footage?" Amber asked with a sly grin.

"Footage?" Dodge asked.

"From the security cameras. Of Stella, in the pond?"

Soon, Dodge would be in the back office with Amber watching the footage of Stella Rubbin in matching black bra and panties, playing in the pond while chugging a large bottle of liquor. He didn't notice when Tilley walked off, as he was too busy watching footage from the morning Charlie Baker died. Amber was much too willing to show him the footage of Stella when she got the news of Charlie's death. The staff had compiled it into a montage and had been sharing it amongst themselves ever since. The montage cleared Stella Rubbin of any wrongdoing, so Dodge asked for a copy. Amber reluctantly sent it to him.

"Just please don't get me fired, okay?" Amber stated.

With Dodge busy with Amber, Tilley wandered off in search of Emma or Bill. They had every intention of questioning Stella, and since that didn't seem quite as important anymore she went in search of someone she felt still might have been holding back information. And with Stella out of commission they had to be here, thought Tilley. Emma had volunteered much in their first conversation but then had divulged much more in their next visit. She couldn't help but wonder what else her old babysitter might have to say. Plus, if she was right about Emma, she would still be conducting therapy sessions, for the juicy gossip more than anything. And if she was right, with an important and willing ear to listen, Tilley suspected that Emma might be the type to say more than she should under these circumstances. The older Emma grew, the stronger her love of gossip seemed to be.

Wandering down an ornate hallway, Tilley heard some-one calling out to her. The voice was not a young one. She peeked into a room where a circle of six mature women sat in uncomfortable padded wooden chairs, each of them knitting something colourful. She recognized the one unnaturally-looking redhead as Myrtle, but the rest of them were white- and grey-haired.

"See," Mavis said as she sat hunched over slightly while knitting. Her dress had multicoloured cat hairs all over it from her two cats. "I told you it was that Tilley girl." She was the oldest of the ladies and had the thickest glasses, but still had managed to recognize her. "I remember her. But last time I saw her she was barely out of diapers." A slight exaggeration on her part, but it had been a very long time since Mavis had set eyes on little "Silly Tilley".

A confused-looking Tilley scanned the group of very familiar ladies. She wasn't sure she knew or remembered most of them but was now certain they knew her.

"She's all grown up now; just like Emma said she was. Her momma would be proud of her," Aunt Agatha added as she blushed, lifted her knitting and worked away feverishly at a purple mitten, avoiding eye contact with Tilley.

"You haven't returned my calls," Tilley said to Agatha.

"I'm sorry, but I was too embarrassed," Agatha blurted, still focused on her knitting.

"She should be, too," Myrtle quipped with a wide grin, exposing her dentures.

"I heard Charlie had a really big one," Ester said. A few

of the others were knitting slippers while she was knitting a small deformed mitten with a too-large thumb.

"We're the Naughty Knitters Club," Geraldine said with a smile, who Tilley now remembered as the wife of Pastor George. Tilley was a little surprised to see her here with this group of ladies.

"A really big one," Ester said with a grin as she focused on her knitting.

"Did you come here to see Stella?" Emma questioned.

Before Tilley could answer the question, Dodge walked in to hear Agatha speak.

"I'm old not dead, you know. My VCR is broken, and I don't know how to work a danged computer," Agatha blurted.

"I could help you with that," Myrtle said with a gentle smile. "And I'll show you the best websites," she added with a wink at Tilley.

"How big was he?" Ester asked, who had now put her knitting down in her lap and was smiling at Dodge.

The slightly flushed Geraldine smiled while looking Dodge up and down as she spoke. "I bet he can still get it up."

Dodge blushed.

Tilley smirked.

"You need help, Ester!" Mavis said.

"Isn't that what we're all here for?" Myrtle quipped with a smile.

"This is a therapy group for sex addicts," Mavis said. She smiled from behind her knitting and winked at Dodge.

"I heard it was a foot long," Ester said as she took to her knitting again. "Like the sandwich."

"Like I said to the cop at the station, the cute one with the broad shoulders and tight butt," Agatha said as she blushed. "When I looked in that morning he was already dead."

"Did you see anyone coming or going that morning?" Tilley asked.

"Cumming?" Myrtle asked with a giggle.

"Not really," Agatha replied. "But I always do my housework in the mornings."

"Naked," Ester said. She checked out Dodge from the corner of her eye as she knitted. "She vacuums and cleans the house naked."

A familiar jingle suddenly sent Myrtle into a frenzied search through her purse. She pulled out a large pink rhinestone-encrusted iPhone and tapped away furiously at it until the resonating sound ceased. With arthritic hands, she fumbled the phone for a moment and then smiled.

"I have to go, ladies," Myrtle said with a smile.

Ester looked at Tilley, scrunched her nose, and smiled as she spoke. "Myrtle got a booty call."

Myrtle's face flushed as she stuffed her knitting equipment into a large flower-printed canvas bag, excused herself, and left the room.

"We'll still need to talk to you some more," Tilley told Agatha as she glanced at the other ladies. "But it might be best if we did it in private at the station."

"Do it here," Ester said. "We want to hear all about it." She smiled at Dodge as she finished knitting what Dodge thought was the ugliest misshapen mitten he'd ever seen.

"We really should go now," Dodge said.

"Here," Ester said, winking, and handed her freshly knitted piece to Dodge. "That's for you. Let me know if it fits. If not, I'm available for private fittings," she added with a smile.

As Dodge and Tilley left the room, Geraldine spoke. "I bet he can still get it up, no problem."

A comment to which Ester replied, "I'd rock his world, twice over."

They could hear the Naughty Knitters giggling like school girls as the detectives left the room. Once out of earshot, Dodge looked at Tilley while showing her what he now held in his hand. "Maybe she should give up knitting," Dodge said as he showed Tilley what the old lady had given him. "That's quite a deformed mitten."

"Actually that's no mitten," Tilley said with a smile. "That's a penis cozy."

Clearly embarrassed, Dodge stuffed the knitted item into his pocket before anyone else could see it as Tilley got a serious case of the giggles that lasted longer than it should have. Tilley wanted revenge for the Charlie's Angels jokes and seized the opportunity to have a good laugh at the expense of her partner. Tilley would have to remind Dodge that the not so innocent group of mature ladies who referred to themselves as the Naughty Knitters were actually a sex therapy group run by Emma O'Brien. That's why they met at the Magnolia Wellness and Rehabilitation Centre.

18

On the way back to the station in Dodge's old rusty Ford Escape, Tilley's iPhone rang. Seeing it was Lemkie she answered the call, putting the phone on speaker so Dodge could hear.

"Hey, got anything for us?" she asked before Lemkie could say anything. She glanced at Dodge while he drove.

"Yes and no," Lemkie replied.

"Why am I not surprised? I should know better than to expect a straight answer from you," replied Tilley with a smirk meant for Dodge.

"Well, it's not what we found but rather what we didn't find," Lemkie replied.

"Spill it," Dodge blurted.

"Well, we went through the entire apartment. Catalogued what looked important, but we went through just about every inch of the place."

"Every inch? You went over every inch?" Tilley replied

with a smile.

"No dick jokes," Lemkie said. "Please no more dick jokes."

"Okay," Dodge said. "But only if you tell us what you didn't find."

"Keys," Lemkie replied. "We never found Charlie's keys."

"Which probably means that's how the killer would have locked the door on her way out," Dodge said.

"Her?" Tilley asked. "You're so damned sure it was a woman. How can you be so sure it wasn't a jealous ex or husband?"

"He was tied to the bed and stiff as a board," Dodge replied.

"Yeah," Lemkie added. "I found nothing to indicate that Charlie liked men and a hell of a lot of evidence to show he really liked women."

"Yeah, sure!" Tilley said. "But what if a jealous husband came by while Charlie was pilled up and helpless? That's possible, if you ask me."

"Sure," Dodge said. "I do admit it's a possibility, but my money's on a woman being the killer. I mean, it could have even happened by accident. Doesn't mean the killer meant to kill Charlie. Perhaps a kinky game that went too far or something."

"Interesting the way your mind works," Tilley replied with a sly grin.

"Can I tell you both something without you guys getting mad?" Lemkie asked.

"I don't like the sound of this," Dodge quipped.

"Shoot," Tilley said, giving Dodge a puzzled look.

"A few of us... well, not us but people at the station... have, uh, started talking about a pool of sorts."

"A what?" Dodge asked.

"You're betting on who the killer is?" Tilley asked. "Seriously?"

"Well, not really," Lemkie replied. "But the idea has been

tossed around some and it's gaining popularity."

"Well, I sure as hell hope this doesn't get to the chief or out to anyone outside the station," Dodge said. "If the mayor, or better yet the press got a hold of this, shit would hit that fan everybody keeps talking about. We've managed to keep most of this out of the press so far and I'd like to keep it that way."

"The press!" Tilley said. "Just imagine if the Naughty Knitters Club got a hold of this juicy piece of gossip."

"The what?" Lemkie asked.

"Long story," Dodge replied.

"Well, don't leave me hanging," Lemkie said.

"I'll fill you in when we get back to the station," Tilley said. "We'll be there soon." She ended the call.

"You want to place a bet, don't you?" Dodge asked as he shot a quick glance at Tilley before turning his attention to his driving again.

"Not just yet," Tilley said. "I have a feeling our list of suspects is not really complete."

"Me, too," Dodge replied. "So, what do you think happened? I mean, why would the killer bother locking the door on her way out?"

"My money is to buy time. I mean, he or she just killed Charlie and probably wanted to get as far away as possible. Maybe even solidify an alibi of some sort in the process."

"Buy time?" Dodge asked, wanting his younger, less experienced partner to fill in the blanks before he did it for her like he often did in the beginning of their collaboration.

"Well, it's obvious Charlie Baker was pretty popular in some circles," Tilley said. "For sure he or she expected someone to show up. I mean, someone did, right?"

"Ms. Weatherbee," Dodge said, glancing at Tilley.

"Weatherbee rang the doorbell but I'm sure not all of Charlie's "friends" would have," Tilley said.

"True," Dodge said as he pulled into the parking lot of

the station and parked his Ford Escape in his usual spot.

Shortly after making coffee, Tilley was telling Lemkie about the ladies who referred to themselves as the Naughty Knitters. She explained to both Dodge and Lemkie how the O'Briens had started the Wellness Centre with only one licensed therapist. Around the same time, Emma would embark on a path to becoming a licensed therapist herself, specializing in sexual therapy. The clinic prospered. Dodge couldn't help but wonder how nosy Emma could be a licensed therapist with her own gossip group and still manage to keep this all quiet enough to keep this a secret. Secret enough that the detective and Head Crime Scene Investigator investigating a Panty Bandit wouldn't know about her role at the centre as a sexual therapist. There had been somebody breaking into homes and stealing women's panties in this town not so long ago, and nobody had thought to tell him the rehab centre treated more than just drugs and alcohol addictions.

Tilley would later confess that she had questioned one of Emma's on-staff therapists about the Panty Bandit behind her partner's back. More or less had consulted the therapist more as profiler, also in hopes that if she had anything she might break her patient-therapist trust and divulge what she knew, woman to woman. But this had been pointless, as the therapist and Emma had known nothing. Although, according to the therapist she spoke with, Emma was very happy to take some wild guesses as to who the Bandit could be. Emma's guesses were so wild that most were preposterous and unfounded. This was why Tilley went to the therapist and not Emma directly. She knew Emma would try to find out who their suspects were. But if anyone at the clinic knew anything, they were lying and wouldn't actually divulge facts if they had them.

Besides, Dodge was still considered new in town back then and had been on the suspect list as well. A fact that insulted his pride at first, but soon had him laughing so hard he almost passed out. He got it. He was new in town around the time the break-ins started. He was often seen out at night and Tilley knew nothing about his nightly runs at that time. It made perfect sense that they thought of him for it, he thought. And by the end of the day, Dodge had already forgiven his partner for going behind his back in the Panty Bandit case. Besides, it had led nowhere, as the Bandit was never caught.

19

Dodge watched as Tilley crossed the street and came to join him in his screened porch. This practice had become somewhat of a routine of theirs at this point. Sometimes they discussed the day's events, if they had interesting cases in progress. But usually they just chatted and got to know each other.

It was on this very porch, during the Panty Bandit case, that Dodge had first told Tilley about how he hadn't lost his virginity until college. The conversation got pretty intense as he told her about his college affair with a much older woman.

He also told her about when he was a teenager; his mature neighbour had caught him looking at her granddaughter. He'd been sixteen at the time and had a crush on the granddaughter who was in some of his classes. But it was her grandmother who had flirted with him every chance she got and the flirting went on for years. But even at an awkward young age Dodge was learning to read people, and he knew she enjoyed teasing him, flirting with him. Part of him also thought it was to keep him away from her granddaughter. She probably didn't want to become a great-grandmother just yet and flirting with him was her way of trying to avoid that. He would never really know, as he had been too embarrassed to ask her then, and she had passed away while he was in the police academy. But to this day he still dreamed of those teenage days when he would visit his neighbour, only to be teased and tormented by the grandmother.

At the time, Tilley had suggested he talk to someone at the clinic. She had mentioned that perhaps Emma could help. The Naughty Knitters had revived these memories for Dodge. Tilley thought this was very funny, but vowed to never repeat any of it. And while Dodge had confessed much in those times spent in the porch, neither of them really knew why he felt he could or should. He had done so anyway, as a strange friendship had developed between them. Perhaps it had been the strange cases they worked together; someone stealing women's underwear from homes all over town. And now this new case where a man is killed in such a strange way.

Tilley, on the other hand, felt reluctant to share like Dodge had done. She did, in the past, reveal to Dodge about her first kiss at the tender age of twelve. The boy had been thirteen and had put his hand on her budding young breast and she had blackened his eye for it. Thinking about how Emma had said she suspected Dodge might be the Panty Bandit Tilley had felt awkward about sharing, even if she thought Emma was off her rocker even back then. Sharing such intimate details with someone like Dodge, who she would always see as her mentor, wasn't something she could be comfortable with.

Tonight Dodge sat in running shorts and t-shirt with his laptop, as usual while nursing a cold beer.

"Anything interesting on Facebook tonight?" Tilley asked as she opened a beer of her own and sat down.

"Nope. But I managed to get a copy of the coroner's report on Charlie Baker."

"Let me guess," Tilley said. "Death by asphyxiation?"

"Yes," Dodge replied. "But he has a theory about the flag

pole."

Tilley laughed sharply before speaking. "Men and their fascination with dicks—it's simply amazing."

"What?" said Dodge with a stupid grin as he took a sip of beer before continuing to explain what would turn out to be a guess more than anything. "Blood clots. He thinks it was blood clots. Apparently our Charlie used to take a lot of blood thinners because of complications from an operation to remove a kidney, years ago. But he wasn't taking them anymore. Probably because of the Viagra."

"That's a lot of maybes, if you ask me."

"Oh, I know," replied Dodge. "But other than Viagra, there was nothing else in his system. No drugs or toxins."

"Asphyxiation," said Tilley.

"Asphyxiation by application of a pillow to face," replied Dodge.

"Was there ever any doubt?" asked Tilley.

"Not really," replied Dodge. "But I was curious as hell about the tent pole."

"I see that," replied Tilley, amusing them both.

"Weren't you?" asked Dodge, remembering how his partner had been mesmerized. How she had stared at it. Now he found himself wondering how long it had been since Tilley had gotten some. He never did see any cars at her house. No gentleman callers since he'd been in town. Rumors at the station were that she'd had a fling with a fellow officer, but nobody offered him any details and he didn't feel he had been around long enough to ask.

His smiled widened as Tilley muttered something he couldn't quite understand as she got up and left, taking her beer with her. She had said something about men being something or other, he wasn't sure. Dodge finished his beer and added it to an almost full bag and tied it loosely, as it wasn't yet ready for Walter's next pick-up.

20

Pegged to a corkboard in the management's office of the Poplar Malls Shopping Centre is a set of keys which have yet to be claimed by anyone. Nor will they ever be since their owner lies on a slab in the morgue. The keys were found in a puddle in the parking lot and had nothing special to help identify them. They contained four keys on a simple ring. Three of the keys had to be house keys, the last perhaps to a padlock or something. At least that's what the mall janitor thought when he found them. Nobody would ever know this was a key Charlie Baker stole from Stella Rubbin. A key to a cabinet where she sometimes kept confiscated materials, including pills. Stella had never noticed when the key went missing because she had a spare in her purse. But nobody would ever know because the keys would remain on the corkboard for nearly two months before being thrown away during one of the janitor's decluttering sprees.

21

The battered laptop lay open, face-down on the dew-covered lawn of the bright yellow house on Robin Street. Very early that morning, while nobody was watching, it had been tossed from a passing car. It bounced on impact once, twirling in the air, causing it to open and land screen-down. A curious crow pecked at it not long after and flew away after quickly losing interest. Ms. Langley, the elderly owner of the home, never noticed the new would-be lawn ornament.

Tuesdays Walter did his usual pick-ups, including the ones on Robin Street. He stopped his tricycle in front of a blue house and collected a full transparent blue bag of cans, plastic bottles, and jugs. The trailer hooked to the back of his tricycle was nearly full and he would have to go to the recycling depot to drop off his first load soon. Today was a good day, thought Walter as he spied the small bag of recyclables Ms. Langley had left out for him. She normally didn't have much but she was more than willing to give them to poor Walter, the brain-damaged boy. He smiled slightly, pleased by the thought as he scooped up the bag and tucked it into the front basket of his tricycle. He wiped his nose with the sleeve of his jacket and said the word Tuesday to nobody in particular. But before Walter could get on his tricycle, something caught his eye as the rising sun reflected off the dew-covered laptop.

"Tuesday," Walter exclaimed for a second time as he walked over to the laptop. He paused and looked around to see if anyone was watching. He was no longer the sharp kid he once had been, and even he realized that. But his mind was deteriorating since the surgery; and the connection from his mind to his mouth seemed broken.

"Tuesday," he said again as he crouched down and turned the laptop over. He poked at the keys like he remembered doing so in the past, but nothing happened. Walter picked up the laptop and examined it closer, seeing its casing was cracked in a few places and it was missing the caps lock and the 'w' key. Otherwise it looked somewhat intact, but even Walter could tell it had been discarded. Unsure why he felt the need to he took it to his tricycle, moving the bags of cans from the front basket to the back basket. He placed the battered laptop in the front basket. He glanced around to see if anyone was watching before heading off on his way to continue his route.

O'Neil, the manager of the recycling centre, tried to take the laptop from Walter when he made his drop of recyclables, but the brain-damaged young man would have none of it. O'Neil went as far as to offer him ten dollars for the laptop but Walter wouldn't part with it. O'Neil stopped pestering when he saw that Walter was getting angry with him.

This wasn't like Walter. He was usually very willing to part with his recyclables, or anything else he might have found, for money. Walter took the payout for the cans and stuffed it into his pocket, climbed on his tricycle, and rode off. Again, this was odd behaviour for Walter, as he always paid close attention to the counting of his haul and made sure he wasn't being ripped off when it came to his money.

"What was that about?" the elderly man asked as he took recyclables from the trunk of his car and carried them to the bay door where O'Neil stood.

"I have no idea," O'Neil replied as he took his hat off, scratched his balding head, and put the hat back on. "I've never seen Walter so flustered before."

"That's that kid who had the brain tumour, isn't it?" the old man asked.

"Yup," O'Neil replied. "He was pretty smart before he had that operation." Truth be told, Walter wasn't that smart before but to O'Neil he had been a whiz kid.

"That's what I hear," the elderly man replied, whom O'Neil remembered as Royal Crown. O'Neil was terrible with names. Royal Crown got his nickname because of the large amount of empty Royal Crown whiskey bottles the old man returned on a regular basis. But O'Neil knew Walter's name. Everybody knew Walter's name.

22

Emma sat in her usual spot on her porch, right next to Bill, a pair of fresh, steaming cups of tea resting on the small table between them. Bill sat with his binoculars, watching what was happening across the street, while Emma gossiped on her freshly charged cordless phone.

"Sadie Cross just came by," Emma said to Myrtle on the other end of the line. "She put flowers next to the steps of

Charlie Baker's apartment. Bill says she was crying."

"Do tell," Myrtle replied, her tone full of intrigue. "You'll have some juicy gossip for our afternoon meeting."

"Her husband's gay, you know," Emma said, as if she had not even heard Myrtle. Emma got excited when she had juicy gossip which she could share. Gossip her clients weren't paying to have kept secret was open for discussion and discuss she would. But the townsfolk were fair game.

Bill lowered his binoculars, fingering wax out of his ear as he gave Emma a funny look as if to make sure he had heard her correctly. Bill was a bit oblivious to this sort of thing. Personality quirks were his wife's thing, not his.

"Poor Sadie wasn't getting any so she was fucking Charlie Baker," Emma said as she gave her husband a sly grin. The same grin she always gets when she has really juicy gossip. "Her car was at Charlie's place often." Truth was, it wasn't there as often as she insinuated, but that didn't matter to Emma.

"Her husband must have known," Myrtle replied.

"I think he was jealous," Emma said. "Probably because he wanted to have sex with Charlie, too."

"Oh, my. You think maybe he killed Charlie?" Myrtle asked. "I heard he was the jealous type, gay or not."

"Naw," Emma replied. "Oh, and there are more flowers, but we don't know who left those."

"Do they look store-bought?" Myrtle asked.

"Bill said he didn't think so, but he doesn't know anything about flowers anyway."

"Agatha's gonna be mad when she sees women are leaving flowers at her apartment building," Myrtle stated with a slightly suppressed chuckle. "Pissed!"

"Oh, I know," Emma replied with a gleeful giggle. She didn't suppress her amusement at all.

"Anyway, the real reason I called was to tell you that I'm gonna have to cancel this afternoon's meeting," Emma added, clearly referring to the group of Naughty Knitters.

"I assumed you were calling about that," Myrtle replied. "I heard Stella's gone and got drunk again. Fell right off the wagon... again."

"Fell off? She hadn't gotten back on it yet," Emma replied. "But that's not the best part."

"Oh, doooo tell," Myrtle replied enthusiastically.

"I heard they found her passed out drunk," Emma said. "And you'll never guess where."

"Oh, spit it out, you old cow!" Myrtle replied.

"They found her in the morgue," Emma said. "She was wrapped in a blanket, lying on the slab with Charlie Baker's body. She had a big empty bottle of vodka and a baggie full of gummy bears."

"Oh, my stars!" Myrtle replied.

"She was so cold, they thought she was dead," Emma replied. "Scared the shit out of the guy who found her when she moved."

Myrtle took to laughing.

"No, I mean it; he actually shit himself. At least that's what I was told."

Both women laughed at this and then Emma continued. "The police are holding her, but I don't think they know what to do with her. I hear they can't decide what to charge her with, if anything at all."

"Poor Stella," Myrtle replied, who didn't really sound all that sympathetic.

"I called them this morning because I want them to send her to the rehab centre, but they said they couldn't just yet."

"I'll call the girls to cancel today's session," Myrtle said.

"See if they want to have it tonight," Emma directed. "Ask them and let me know."

Bill lowered his binoculars and gave Emma a dirty look that she knew meant that he didn't approve of them meeting that night. He didn't approve because they had plans that night that involved being home alone. Plans that now had to change because Emma had juicy gossip that couldn't be put off too long, as juicy gossip only stayed juicy for so long. Juicy gossip had a short lifespan and a fast approaching expiration date. His plans would have to wait until Emma was good and ready, as usual. Nothing much he could say about that. He sneered at Emma, sipped some tea, and then went back to his binoculars. Emma ended her call with Myrtle and then dialled another number. She just had to call Agatha and see if she knew about the flowers being left at the bottom of the steps of the late Charlie Baker's old apartment. A part of her hoped Agatha didn't know, so she could be the one to tell her. Emma smiled as Agatha picked up the call.

"You'll never guess what I'm looking at," Emma exclaimed to Agatha.

"What now?" Agatha replied in frustration as Emma burst into giggles.

23

"Where the hell were you?" Trudy barked as she closed the bedroom door so her daughter couldn't hear them.

"I texted you earlier that I had a last-minute showing to do," Marci replied as she slipped off her battered, brown leather driving gloves while Trudy watched angrily.

Trudy hated those stupid brown driving gloves. Marci always dressed sexily, which was one of the things that had attracted Trudy to Marci the most. Before they had started seeing each other Marci had always come to Trudy's office in tight business suits, showing off her curves and those long legs. But those stupid driving gloves always clashed with the outfits and Trudy hated them. She even bought her a new pair of black leather gloves. Marci had thanked her for them. Then she had proceeded to tuck them away in her underwear drawer and kept on wearing those stupid battered ones. Marci never admitted to Trudy that the black gloves she had given her were cheap, stiff imitation leather and so she didn't like them.

"That was two hours ago!" Trudy screamed. "You know I worry."

"I know," Marci replied. "But you don't need to."

"You're cheating on me, aren't you?" Trudy asked, tears running down her face.

"You know that's not true," Marci replied. "I flirt, yes. But you of all people knew that when you and I started seeing each other."

"I know," Trudy said.

"It makes me feel good," Marci said, referring to her flirtatious nature. She faced Trudy and gripped her shoulders. Trudy, who was already shorter than her lover, shrunk a little in her grasp as Marci spoke on. "Flirting makes me feel alive. I can't help it."

"I know that but I just wish I was enough for you."

"You are more than enough. I flirt but I'd never cheat on you."

"How am I supposed to know that?" Trudy replied.

Marci hooked her fingers in Trudy's waistband, pulled her close, and kissed her passionately. She did this before Trudy could say another word. Marci was tired of fighting.

24

A small sign sat in the front window just under the big red letters that read *Vernon's Meats*. The small white, neatly hand-printed sign read *Sale on Sausages*. Vernon was behind the counter in a blood-stained apron, talking to a customer about his hand-made sausages and how he had a secret combination of spices that made them like nothing else on the market. His secret was really some spices and a red wine marinade and not even his wife knew that. The only person who knew this was his accountant because he saw the receipts for the wine and had asked about it. That's when Vernon told his accountant that if he mentioned this to anyone about the wine marinade, he would kill him. And kill him he would and make sausages out of his fat ass. Vernon was a burly, imposing man, and although he would never hurt a fly the accountant got the distinct impression that Vernon might just have meant that threat, and so it was best to keep the butcher's secret. It's always a good idea to be nice to the man with the big, sharp knives who carved meat for a living.

Sadie walked in, clutching her large purse to her side, and went directly to the freezer where Vernon kept the meat pies he made using his late mother's recipe. She took out a beef pie, looked at it sourly, and exchanged it for a chicken meat pie instead.

"Hey, hon," Vernon said in his gravelly voice. "What are you doing here at this hour?"

Sadie knew exactly what he meant as she watched the older lady whom he had been serving walk past her and leave with her purchases. He was wondering why she wasn't at the daycare, tending to the kids, where she ought to be.

"I left early," Sadie replied. "I wasn't feeling well."

"Is that supper?" Vernon asked, gesturing to the meat pie Sadie was holding.

"I just told you I'm not feeling well and so I really don't feel like cooking."

"There was an article with a picture of flowers in front of Charlie Baker's place in the paper this morning."

"What are you saying?" Sadie asked.

"Remi, our neighbour, told me he saw you leaving flowers at Charlie Baker's place this morning."

"So?" Sadie asked.

Vernon was nonplussed at Sadie's lack of reaction. "People are talking, Sadie."

"I don't give a royal shit what people think anymore," she barked.

Vernon was a little surprised by how blunt Sadie was being. She was always the meek little mouse when in public, but she hadn't been herself since that Charlie Baker died. Sure, he knew she had been sleeping with Charlie. But he would never have said anything. Vernon was the type who was always concerned about what people thought, and so giving them fodder for gossip was not something he wanted to do. Plus, while she was sneaking out to see Charlie, Vernon had been sneaking out, too, to hook up with a man named Dave he'd met on a website.

"But, honey, think about the kids," Vernon replied, who knew damned well this was her weakness. The kids at the daycare were her life; especially since they had never had any of their own. He knew she would be more concerned about them being affected than anything else. He knew their old understanding that reputations could affect both their businesses was a thing of the past for Sadie now.

"I'm not feeling well," Sadie stated, in a serious tone. "I'm going home to lie down."

"You ate too much chocolate," Vernon quipped as he watched her clutch her purse a little tighter when he said that. "That's why you don't feel well."

They both knew he was right. Sadie ate chocolate when she was upset. She had switched to dark chocolate years ago because she could say it was good for her, an excuse she used constantly to help justify it.

Sadie turned and walked towards the door, paused, and whirled around quickly. With one swift motion, she threw the frozen meat pie at her husband. Vernon ducked and the frozen pie made a loud cracking noise as it hit the wall behind him and then crashed to the floor. By the time Vernon felt it was safe to peek from behind the counter again, he saw the glass door closing behind his wife. She got in her car, slammed the door, and squealed the tires as she pulled out of the parking lot.

25

Frustrated at the progress of the case, Tilley had left the station early and was on the hunt again. Only this time she was on the hunt for the perfect grapefruit. She groped, gently squeezed, shook, and smelled them in some strange process of elimination. Finally selecting one that would do, she put it in the small shopping basket that hung in the crook of her arm.

Detective Tilley's best ideas always came to her when she wasn't trying. This case simply had too many potential suspects and nothing to help zero in on any one suspect. This frustrated her to no end. But the most frustrating thing about it was that this didn't seem to bother her partner at all. Detective Franklin Dodge was too calm about everything related to this case and it was starting to get under her skin. Perhaps it was his many more years of experience as a detective, but Tilley wanted leads. Lemkie and Calvin were giving them nothing. Lemkie was too busy making fun of Calvin having to watch hours upon hours of homemade porn. Lemkie had left an arm sling, some topical pain reliever, and a box of tissues on Calvin's desk as a practical joke; although the look on Calvin's face had been sort of funny, thought Tilley. Especially when he actually took the cream for the pain, flipped Lemkie the bird, and walked away. That was funny, thought Tilley. She hadn't even realized she was smiling when she heard a voice that pulled her back to reality.

"What?" Tilley asked as she turned around to see who had spoken.

"I said, what's so funny?" Ms. Weatherbee inquired.

Tilley's smile faded as, in her mind, she heard her old teacher finish that sentence with her patented exclamation of the words, "young lady".

"I was just remembering something," Tilley replied.

Ms. Weatherbee blushed slightly and looked around to see if anyone was within hearing distance.

"Don't you dare make fun of me, young lady!" Ms. Weatherbee said in a firm yet low tone of voice. She picked up a grapefruit of her own and pretended to be examining it carefully, not wanting to make eye contact with her former student.

Realizing that Ms. Weatherbee had thought that Tilley was recalling seeing her at the door to Charlie Baker's apartment, she said, "It was just something a co-worker... never mind."

"I hope you don't think of me as some sort of slut," Ms. Weatherbee said, who was still avoiding eye contact.

"I think you're human," Tilley replied. "At least I think that now," she added with a smile.

Ms. Weatherbee smiled and looked up at Tilley. "He just kept coming on to me. Every time I'd see him in town, he'd flirt with me."

"You don't have to explain yourself to me," Tilley replied, before remembering that she was now the person of authority in this conversation. "Well, actually, maybe you do, but you know what I mean."

"I never slept with him, you know."

Tilley's brow furrowed slightly, as if to ask without asking.

"I mean, I would have that morning."

Tilley said nothing, knowing full well she didn't need to as it was obvious Ms. Weatherbee needed to get this off her chest.

"I mean, a woman does have needs, too," Ms. Weatherbee said as she blushed. "But I'm no whore," she boldly declared.

"I never said..." Tilley started before being cut off mid-sentence.

"I just heard he was so damned good and I was so frustrated!"

Ms. Weatherbee looked down at her hand to see that her fingers and thumb had broken the skin of the grapefruit and its juice was running down her arm.

"Can you tell that Detective Dodge I'm no whore?" Ms. Weatherbee asked as she put the grapefruit back in the pile and wiped her hand on her pants without realizing what she was doing.

"He'll be happy to hear that," Tilley replied.

"Sure," Ms. Weatherbee replied as she looked around to see if anyone could hear them talking.

"I have to ask, though," Tilley replied. "Did you see anything weird that morning? Anything you might consider out of the ordinary?"

"I don't remember," Weatherbee replied. "I was so nervous; I barely remembered flashing you and that partner of yours until I got home."

"Understood," Tilley replied, trying hard not to smile.

Ms. Weatherbee turned to walk away as Tilley spoke.

"Thank you for coming to talk to me," Tilley offered, knowing full well Ms. Weatherbee was no longer listening. She marvelled at how flustered Ms. Weatherbee had looked. She had never seen her like this.

Tilley turned to see Sadie Cross pushing a small shopping cart towards her only to freeze in mid-step and change directions and walk away. In her shopping cart there were six cans of Alphagetti and four giant slabs of dark chocolate. The biggest chocolate bars Tilley had ever seen.

Tilley turned towards the vegetable department and spotted Marci Grant standing in sexy heels, holding a cauliflower in her gloved hands while looking directly at her. Tilley had a moment of self-consciousness, feeling completely exposed, and shuddered at the thought of having Marci looking at her with such intensity.

Then, in the blink of an eye, Trudy emerged and grasped Marci by the arm, dragging her away. Tilley could hear Trudy's tone and it sounded harsh. It sounded like Trudy wasn't pleased at all and was voicing it right there in the Food Emporium, not holding anything back.

"Not making any friends, am I?" Tilley said to herself as she walked off into the produce section.

"No, you're not," Tilley heard coming from behind her where Ester emerged, pushing an empty shopping cart, braced on it for extra support as she walked past. Ester was smiling her little coy smile that told Tilley she had most likely heard the entirety of the conversations, and she couldn't wait to share at the next Naughty Knitters meeting.

26

Calvin plopped himself into his chair, set his newly filled cup of water down, and woke his computer from sleep mode as his phone rang. He typed in his computer password as he answered the call.

"Hey, Tilley," Calvin said, recognizing the number on the phone's display screen. "Where'd you run off to?"

"I needed to think," Tilley replied. "That and I went to get a few things at the grocery store. Hey, are you still compiling pictures from Charlie Baker's hard drive?"

"Yes, he is," she heard Dodge say.

"Am I on speaker phone?" Tilley asked with frustration in her voice.

"Sorry," Calvin replied. He knew that doing this to Tilley without telling her would seriously upset her, and now he heard it in her tone of voice. "Where are you?" he asked.

"I'm still at the grocery store," Tilley replied.

Dodge retrieved pages from the printer near Calvin's desk. Standing behind Calvin, he said, "Calvin was just printing me some of the pictures he's compiled."

"I'm putting them in a folder for you now," Calvin added.

"That's great," Tilley replied. "Thanks."

"What was it you wanted to know?" Dodge asked.

"Well, let's just say something just happened that made me wonder if a certain redhead was one of the women on that hard drive," Tilley said as she watched Marci Grant and Trudy Wilkins push a shopping cart to a white car. They were too busy being angry with each other to notice the detective watching them.

"Red?" Dodge asked.

"Marci Grant?" Calvin asked. "I didn't find any pics of her."

"Okay," Tilley replied. "It was just a thought."

"Dodge said Charlie wasn't her type," Calvin said, happy to deflect some of the jokes away from him for a change. "He said you were more her type."

Dodge gave Charlie a dirty look that said he wasn't supposed to repeat that, especially not to Tilley. Dodge leafed through the printed pictures before speaking.

"I'm not sure why you'd think that," Dodge replied. "She told us she was talking to him about the Turlington house."

"I know, I was there when she told us," Tilley replied. "I guess I was just wondering if she and Charlie had ever hooked up."

"If they did, I don't think Charlie got it on video," Calvin said. "But there was lots of footage of Lucy Shaffer with Charlie. I think that's what the hackers were after."

"The hackers?" Tilley inquired.

"Calvin was telling me hackers tried to get at the files on his computer," Dodge said.

"The files weren't on it and so they didn't get those." Calvin explained, referring to the extra computer servers he'd set up during the lull after the Panty Bandit case went cold.

"I figure someone wanted to know who Charlie's lady friends were," Dodge said.

"I'm thinking they wanted pictures of Lucy Shaffer with Charlie. Or better yet, video," Calvin said. "A lot of tabloid websites would pay big money for that."

"True," Tilley replied. Lucy Shaffer's career was on a high note after making a few hit movies. Lucy was a red-blooded woman just like all the others, but her being famous made the rumours even juicier. A few tabloid reporters had been seen near the rehab centre, asking questions. She knew Calvin was right about the tabloids paying big money for proof. For a brief second she wondered just how much such evidence might be worth before dismissing the thought.

"Dodge?" Tilley said.

"Yes?" Dodge replied as Calvin looked from the phone to Dodge and back to the phone.

"Did Calvin find any pictures of Ms. Weatherbee?" Tilley smiled as she asked this. She knew Dodge was probably in Calvin's office looking for exactly that.

Dodge flushed slightly but didn't acknowledge the fact that Tilley was right. He was in fact looking to know if Ms. Weatherbee had slept with Charlie Baker. He assumed she had not from the body language she'd displayed on the morning they found the late Charlie Baker. Dodge wanted to know if his young partner's former fifth-grade teacher had known Charlie intimately. He had to know. He was conflicted about this, as finding her picture would mean he would have reason to talk to her. But not the reason he would prefer.

Tilley knew now that they wouldn't find Ms. Weatherbee in the videos, but she wanted to wait a little longer to tell Dodge. He was more than willing to tease her about Marci Grant.

"Are we done here?" Dodge asked as he pulled a picture

of Lucy Shaffer from the folder and placed it on top of the pile.

Once the call was terminated, Dodge returned to his desk and felt a wave of relief wash over him. He sat in his chair and dropped the folder on his desk. Relief was what he found himself feeling after not having found Ms. Weatherbee's picture in the folder; although a thought occurred to him at that moment that they were still missing something. There was a square of missing dust on a shelf that they suspected could have been a laptop. She could be in those videos, he thought. That's when the relief he had felt dissipated as quickly as it had come.

Driving towards the station, Tilley swung past Charlie Baker's apartment and saw that a few more bouquets of flowers had been placed at the bottom of the steps near the yellow police tape. She slowed slightly as she drove past. She looked at the O'Briens' house and figured no one was home. She slowed a little more and looked at the RED Realty sign on the lawn of the Turlington house; the red hair even redder, the teeth even whiter on the sign.

Calvin waited until Dodge was gone to grab a box of tissues and locked himself in the small dark room he had been using to watch all the videos from Charlie Baker's hard drive. Watching all that porn was becoming a serious problem. All Calvin could think about now was sex, and it was starting to affect his work. But the case made it so that he couldn't get away from it. Lemkie was having too much fun with it, too. Calvin hadn't masturbated this much since he was a teenager. With the door locked and the blinds shut, he sat at the monitor. With Lemkie out of the office early that day, he wanted a moment alone to watch the video of Charlie and Stella again. There was one he couldn't get out of his mind. It was hot and he wanted a moment alone to watch it again. But this time he had the tissues.

27

With her car at the shop getting an oil change, Trudy sat in the passenger seat of the older-model red Corvette with the word RED on the vanity plate. Marci sat, gripping the steering wheel with her brown, battered-glove-covered hands. Trudy's eyes wandered over her lover's long legs as she drove, occasionally glancing at the driving gloves with distaste.

"I got an offer on the Turlington place today," Marci said, trying to make conversation to break the awkward silence.

"Was it a lowball offer or a serious one?" Trudy asked.

"Semi-serious," Marci replied.

"Is it gonna sell?"

"Don't know yet. Although it would be pretty sweet if it did."

"My office isn't even done processing the sale you had two weeks ago," replied Trudy as she gazed out the window at the houses they passed on their way to Trudy's office.

Marci knew something was troubling Trudy and she had no doubt what it was. Her demeanour had changed since they had watched *Entertainment Tonight*. The petite blonde hostess with the tight top had said that comedian Lucy Shaffer was back in rehab. This meant she was in town, staying at the Magnolia Wellness and Rehabilitation Centre. And knowing this, Trudy was worried that Marci would hang around there again like the last time Lucy had been in town. Marci was star-struck when it came to Lucy Shaffer. At least that's what she had told Trudy when she found out and confronted her about it. And it didn't matter that Lucy wasn't gay. Trudy didn't care that Lucy liked men. She had been angry that Marci had gone out of her way to bump into Lucy. Her excuse was that she'd heard the comedian wanted to buy a house here in Poplar Falls. And now Lucy Shaffer was back in town and Marci didn't seem to care that Lucy was a heterosexual drunk.

Marci turned down a side street, taking one of her typical detours. She wanted to check out a house for sale by a competitor. She slowed to glance at the competitor's sign on a well manicured lawn of the bright yellow house on Robin Street. Ms. Langley must be moving in with her son after all. At least that was the rumour, as her neighbours were former clients of RED Realty. And from the sounds of it, they weren't too heart-broken on Ms. Langley moving away. She had a reputation with the neighbourhood as the one who called the cops for any little thing that looked odd to her. And to Ms. Langley, that was a long list. Most of the police officers knew her well, including the detectives now on the Charlie Baker case. Marci slowed her car as she drove past, pulling into the middle of the road to avoid the slow kid on his large tricycle and trailer. She slowed the car and looked at Walter and his partially loaded tricycle with a look of disdain that Trudy noticed and commented on.

"What is it with you and this Walter kid?"

"He's a pain in my ass," Marci commented.

"Why? He's harmless."

"You know I have to explain his route to everyone one of my clients that buys a house in his neighbourhoods."

Trudy didn't know what to say to that, as Marci did have a point. Walter's obsession with collecting recyclables was strange; but harmless.

Marci glanced in her rear-view mirror and saw that Walter had a busted laptop in his tricycle's front basket. As she drove on, her brow furrowed in confusion as she wondered what a slow kid like Walter was doing with that in his basket. At least Trudy seemed to be forgetting about this Lucy Shaffer business. This was a relief because Trudy could be like a dog with a bone sometimes. And Lucy was a tasty bone, thought Marci, a small smirk spreading on her lips as she took a turn in the direction of Trudy's office.

28

"Lucy's agent called," Dodge said as he pulled ahead in the drive-thru of a Jabba-da-Java Coffee Hut.

"You serious?" Tilley asked.

"Yup," Dodge replied as he pulled his old, rusty Ford Escape up to the speaker. Not wanting to discuss an ongoing investigation by a drive-thru microphone, Dodge ordered the coffees and waited until he pulled ahead before speaking.

"Anyway, her agent set up a meeting with her for us," Dodge replied.

"Her agent?" Tilley asked. "You'd think she'd call herself."

"Her agent probably advised against that since she's back in rehab again," Dodge said as he dug out his money to pay.

"They both know we don't suspect her anyway, right?" Dodge shrugged. "We can only assume so."

"She was shooting that movie in Las Vegas," Tilley added.

"Her agent asked us not to speak to any press about this," Dodge said as he pulled up to the drive-thru window. He collected the coffees, paid, and drove off before either of them said anything else.

"I heard she started drinking again because of this shit with Charlie," Tilley said, as she found herself wondering what the tabloids would pay for some of those juicy photos of the famous comedian with Charlie Baker. A sly smile spread across her lips as they drove on, headed for the Magnolia Wellness and Rehabilitation Centre.

A short while later, Detectives Dodge and Tilley sat under a small gazebo on the grounds, across from Lucy Shaffer. Lucy hid behind what Dodge thought was the largest and darkest pair of sunglasses he had ever seen. A large white hat shaded the fair-skinned comedian from the morning sun.

She wore a white robe embroidered with the initials MWRC which covered her silk pyjama top, obviously not provided by the Rehabilitation Centre. Both Dodge and Tilley couldn't help but notice all this as Lucy barely looked in their direction as she spoke.

"I'm no whore, I'll have you know," Lucy said. "Yes, okay, I slept with Charlie but not right away or anything. He's a charming... I mean, he was a charming man, you know."

Dodge scribbled something in a notepad as both he and Tilley checked out Lucy's bare crossed legs, a slipper dangling off her right foot.

"Plus I was drunk, the first time. We both were," Lucy added, as she seemed to trail off thinking about Charlie Baker. "Not that being drunk justifies our fling, mind you. He was an amazing lover and an even better listener."

"Was the fling still ongoing?" Tilley asked.

"No," Lucy replied as she still stared off into the distance. "You know he's the only fling I've ever had, and the fucking press is going to paint me out to be some kind of whore."

"Was he seeing anyone else, while you and he were seeing each other?" Tilley asked.

"How should I know?" Lucy replied, and glanced at Tilley only to return her gaze to a woman sipping tea at a table on a nearby balcony. "I bet that's not tea," muttered Lucy before getting back to her story. "Charlie was charming, let me tell you. Most of the women here either loved him or had the hots for him, especially that Stella Rubbin."

"Tell us about Stella." Dodge said as he took more notes.

"I heard they might fire her," Lucy said. "She was so in love with Charlie, but I only found that out after he and I started seeing each other."

A small golf cart drove past the gazebo. The man driving the cart waved at the three of them sitting in the shade. Lucy waved but looked away to hide her face as she did so.

"Look, I don't know who would want to kill Charlie,"

Lucy stated as she finally glanced at each detective before looking off again. "I mean, I could understand some of the women wanting to kill each other over him but..."

Lucy trailed off as a sudden look of panic came over her.

"Fuck," she blurted as she looked down, hiding behind her hat. She pulled a cell phone from her robe pocket, dialled using a single button, and put the phone to her ear.

Tilley and Dodge exchanged glances before realizing that something was clearly upsetting Lucy, and they had an idea of what it might be. Dodge spotted a man ducking behind bushes with what had to be the longest camera lens he had ever seen.

Without another word, Lucy got up and walked off, clearly chewing out whomever she had called. Dodge glanced back to the man in the bushes and recognized him as the driver of the golf cart that had driven past them mere moments before.

At the back door of one of the buildings stood a man dressed all in white, clearly a staff member, who was pointing out the paparazzo to a man in a security guard uniform.

Dodge and Tilley exchanged glances as they watched the man in the bushes duck out of sight, eventually reappearing from behind the bushes in the same golf cart as before. The security guard radioed someone on a shoulder radio.

"You can't outrun a radio," Dodge said with a smirk.

"What?" Tilley asked as she and Dodge walked off the gazebo and onto a perfectly groomed path.

"Just something my brother once told me when we were kids," Dodge replied.

29

Detective Franklin Dodge didn't really consider himself all that smart, especially not when he worked with the likes of Detective Roxanne Tilley, although he'd never tell her that. Although she lacked experience, he knew that she would eventually be the better detective of the two of them, and those days were not that far off. But what he felt he lacked in smarts he made up for in wisdom and keen observational skills. Dodge used to feel he was pretty good at reading people, until he moved to Poplar Falls and met Tilley. Although he figured she did have an unfair advantage there, since she grew up in this quaint little city.

Plus, whenever he did start feeling a bit intelligent, one of those crime scene investigator kids like Lemkie would teach him something new and he was reminded of how he was falling behind in the times. Technology was advancing way too fast for Dodge, and he felt like it was making him into a dinosaur sooner than he would have liked.

Stumped after spending the morning mulling over pictures and ideas with Tilley, Dodge called it quits early. He rose from his desk, stating that he always did some his best thinking after a run and so he would call Tilley if he had any bright ideas. She agreed to do the same.

Now Dodge sat in his Ford Escape, having decided to get a few things on the way home. In the back seat sat a few grocery bags and a case of beer. The beer was what he had really wanted, since it wasn't really the run that helped the ideas flow but the beers he always had afterwards.

He'd bumped into Myrtle while doing his shopping and he smiled at their brief encounter. She had inquired about the investigation (of course) and Dodge had politely told her that he couldn't discuss that with her.

Myrtle said that he didn't have to tell her anything, as everybody in Poplar Falls knew that he and Tilley had met with Lucy Shaffer that day. The pictures were all over Facebook from the tabloid website and that paparazzo guy who'd been hiding in the bushes. Dodge's favourite part of the encounter had been when she winked and blushed, saying that

Mavis and Ester told her to say hello next time she saw that handsome Detective Dodge.

Dodge smiled to himself as he put his key in the ignition but stopped before turning it as something caught his eye. Walter's tricycle and trailer were parked near the front entrance of the grocery store; he'd walked past it on his way out just a few moments ago. But what he hadn't noticed was what sat in the basket on the front of the tricycle. It looked like a battered laptop was sitting wedged in sideways on top of a few empty liquor bottles. At that moment Dodge remembered the dusty imprint on a shelf about the size of a laptop at Charlie Baker's apartment.

"Nah," Dodge said to himself. "Can't be..."

He got out of his truck, leaving the driver's door open without realizing it. He walked to the tricycle in a bit of a daze and gingerly picked up the busted laptop, as if he was afraid of breaking it more. What he was really afraid of was Lemkie giving him shit later about getting his prints all over it. He rotated the laptop, looking it over as if expecting to find something to tell him this was indeed Charlie Baker's computer. This was too good to be true, if it turned out to indeed be the missing laptop he thought, and so there was no way he could leave it there. Looking around to see if anyone was watching and satisfied that no one was, he carried the busted hardware to his car, got in, and placed it on the passenger seat.

Dodge shut the door but sat there, looking at the laptop for a moment, finding himself unable to leave yet and not really sure why. After a few moments, he realized why he felt he couldn't depart. He was waiting for Walter to come out and discover his property was missing. Dodge found himself bothered by the idea, for some strange reason he couldn't understand. Walter was a simple-minded man with brain damage, but Dodge felt sorry for him. And when Walter finally did come out of the Food Emporium carrying a couple of plastic bags containing what looked to be canned goods he paused, standing in front of his tricycle. Dodge watched as Walter dug through one of the bags, felt his pockets as if looking for something, and then placed one of the bags of cans in the front basket without hesitation. The second bag Walter placed in the basket at the back of his tricycle. He checked the hitch to his trailer before clumsily climbing onto his tricycle and beginning to pedal. The thin man in baggy clothes and crooked baseball cap worked hard to get the tricycle moving. Dodge watched him turn and pedal the tricycle in his direction.

Walter looked at Dodge as he rode past the Ford Escape. The detective couldn't hear the brain-damaged young man, but he read his lips as he mouthed the word 'Wednesday' with the best of crooked grins he could manage as he glanced in the direction of the Ford. Dodge looked into the basket and saw cans of pasta, stew, and beans protruding from the bag. At that moment Dodge made a mental note to go visit Walter at his home. At least he would try.

He had heard that Walter's mother wasn't an easy person to get along with, but Dodge decided he would try as he started his car and headed back to the station. He had no way of knowing if his hunch about the busted laptop being Charlie's was right, but he just had to know if it was. Plus, Lemkie was pretty much done processing the rest of the evidence and so he should have time to look at it anyway, Charlie's or not. That's what he thought, as he never fully understood the complexities of the two crime scene investigators. To avoid too many questions he would leave the laptop on Lemkie's desk with a note, asking him to check it out. And if he knew Lemkie, he'd already be on it by the time Dodge got to the station. Lemkie was usually in early, except on the days when he had to drop off his son at the Sunshine and Rainbows Daycare. Either way, Dodge would leave it on his desk with a note to have the laptop looked at it as soon as he could. Please and thank you.

30

Walter smelled bad and he knew it. But while pedaling his way home, he could only focus on the task at hand. The brain tumour and haemorrhage had left Walter with diminished capacities, which meant he was permanently in a one-track mode, being limited to one task at a time. Multitasking was not something Walter would ever get to do again, as that was a thing of the past. There was a time when Walter would have been able to fend for himself without his mother to remind him of everything. But that ability had been cut out and thrown into an incinerator by a well-meaning doctor who saved his life yet had sentenced Walter to a life as a simpleton at the same time. The irony was that Walter hadn't been the nicest person before the surgery. He would have laughed at and made fun of people who were like he now was. He used to know better than to vocalize any of his insensitivity around his mother, as she would have beaten some sense into him. But now the irony, which was lost on the young man, was that Walter was what he used to find funny. And his mother wouldn't have beaten him at all after the tumour.

Walter's mother was a shut-in who lived off a disability pension; she hardly left the house and was rarely seen, except for her occasional trips to the grocery store. She wasn't a mean person, but Walter was always afraid of her. Her fierce temper was matched only by her powerful love for her son. She coddled and protected him even when he should have been old enough to leave the house. For those reasons moving out had never crossed his mind, and once the tumour came that option was taken off the table forever. He depended on his mother more and more as time went on, though for the past seven months she hadn't reminded Walter to bathe, or to put his clothes in the wash. A few neighbours had tried to ask Walter about his mother, noticing her lack of trips to the grocery store, but Walter had only been able to respond in his usual manner, muttering the day of the week and struggling to smile.

As the sun was setting, Walter arrived at the trailer he called home and drove his tricycle into the darkness of the open shed. The door had been half torn off its hinges in a wind storm and Walter had never been able to shut it since. Guided by the moonlight, Walter took the grocery bags full of cans from the tricycle baskets and went through the unlocked front door. Walter didn't bother taking his shoes off as he went inside the smelly trailer, his nose long ago having become accustomed to the stench. He made his way past some clutter to the brightly lit kitchen and set the bags on the dirty, cluttered, fly-specked counter top. He stood before the cupboards, which had many drawers and doors standing open, and stared at the bags and the clutter for a few moments, as if processing what he should do next. After nearly two minutes of contemplation, Walter opened a bottom cabinet door and removed a wrinkled garbage bag and began taking empty cans from the counter top and putting them into the bag. He took the bag outside and into the back yard, where he emptied the trash bag at the top of a sloping lawn. The cans nosily tumbled down the embankment to settle at the bottom with the rest of the trash that lay at the base of some wild brush. He pocketed the crumpled trash bag and urinated outside before going back inside, putting the bag where he had gotten it, under the cupboards. He paused again, but only for a moment this time as his growling stomach reminded him what he needed to do next. Eat. Walter was hungry and his mother wasn't there to cut the crusts off his sandwiches anymore, let alone make him one of his favourite dishes. Walter looked at the caked dirty pot that still sat in the sink, rinsed but never actually washed. Mould had grown on it over time.

"Thursday," Walter muttered. A tear streaked down his cheek as he remembered his mother's beef stew. He unpacked the groceries, which consisted of canned goods only: pastas, stews, and other various things that had appealing pictures on the labels. He placed most of the cans on the counter top and a few in an already opened cupboard. He took one of the cans and reached for the electric can opener and then paused partway. He remembered how the can opener no longer worked and so took the manual one from the already open drawer on his right. After some struggle, Walter managed to remove the lid of the can enough to get at the food inside. He took a dirty spoon from the countertop, wiped it on his shirt, and took a spoonful of the Irish stew from the can and shakily put it in his mouth. He was famished. He stared at the dark microwave with longing as he ate the cold stew.

Walter had forgotten he wasn't supposed to put the can in the microwave and thrown the breaker for the kitchen outlets long ago. None of the electrical appliances worked anymore. The old Walter would have gone to the electrical panel in his bedroom, the one behind the cheap wooden cupboard door, and thrown the breaker back on. Even though now that would have been pointless, he still would have tried it. But the new Walter couldn't even remember where the breaker box was, let alone make the mental connection between the lack of electricity and the wood panel behind the door of his bedroom. Without his mother, he couldn't manage these things anymore. He couldn't even remember his mother making him run those wires that meant a few things still worked even if the trailer had no electricity anymore. She had him do this a month before his surgery to save money on electricity. Now those wires were the only reason he still had what he had. And on a good day he might remember something about that, but those good days were rare now.

Walter felt his stomach calm down as he finished his can of Irish stew. He placed the empty can on the cupboards, supplying the flies something new to investigate. He licked and sucked the spoon as clean as he could and placed it at the exact spot he had retrieved it.

He made his way to his bedroom but paused before a cluttered freezer on the way. Strewn about on top of the freezer was a pile of papers and junk mail, most of which was unopened. Amidst this clutter was an out-of-place, large, battered box. Walter clumsily cracked open the box and set the lid aside as he reached into his pockets. He removed all of the money he had left from his day's work collecting cans and looked at it. He looked in the box, which contained coins and bills that sat on a red silk cloth that peeked out in between the money. The last time Walter tried to count his money to see if he had enough, he had gotten so flustered and confused that he had left the box open and had not gone on his usual recycling collections for two full days. He looked at the thirty-three dollars and forty-five cents with certainty even though he forgot that he paid for groceries with some of it. He was pretty sure O'Neil hadn't ripped him off today.

He put the money in the box with the rest of the cash and didn't bother putting the lid on the box. He was tired and didn't know how long he could keep this up. Being a moron was exhausting, thought Walter. He had a sense of who he had become, but he couldn't form a proper train of thought to figure all this out. He knew he needed to wash his clothes and try and wash himself, but that would have to wait until the morning. If he remembered by then. And washing to Walter was going to consist of rinsing out his clothes and standing under a cold shower for a few minutes. No soap would be used on either the clothes or himself, but he would be satisfied with his efforts. These thoughts crossed his mind but were fleeting as he climbed onto his bed, fully clothed, and dragged a large, heavy, dirty blanket on top of himself.

Walter was asleep the moment he settled himself under his blanket.

Walter wept softly in his sleep as he dreamt of his mother, but he wouldn't remember the dreams come morning. Only that he would need to eat more stew and go collect more bottles and cans. Walter had good days and bad days, but the good days were rare now and getting scarcer as time passed.

July

31

"I'm sorry, ma'am, but I can't divulge that information," the young woman said from behind the front desk of the Magnolia Wellness and Rehabilitation Centre. She wore the clerical staff's dark burgundy-coloured uniform with a gold nametag that read 'Amber', and Amber's patience was clearly wearing thin. It was way too early in the morning for this, she thought, as she forced a smile that was starting to look painful.

"Like I told Dale, I have an appointment with Lucy Shaffer at 8:30," Marci Grant said. "He was smart enough to let me in," she added, normally a very convincing liar. Although the truth was that Dale had let her in because she had worn her low-cut blouse and red blazer. Armed with this, she had flashed him some cleavage and leg and got poor Dale flustered and confused. He had made what he quickly realized was the wrong decision by opening the gate so that Marci could drive onto the grounds. Dale had already been dreading the chewing-out he would get while he had watched the older model red Corvette with the word RED on the vanity plate disappear behind the closing entrance gate.

Amber, still smiling her best placating smile, looked Marci up and down, thinking that Marci was dressed to impress, although perhaps with too much sex appeal for most. The red blazer and matching skirt suited her well, but the battered brown leather driving gloves looked out of place to Amber. The Wellness Center employee spoke as calmly as she could manage under the circumstances.

"Look, Miss Grant, you try something like this every time Miss Shaffer is in town, okay?" Amber's smile was finally replaced by a stern look.

"I'm not sure what you mean," Marci replied, with what some might consider an award-wining performance. "She told me that next time she was in town, she wanted to look at some properties—in the more upscale part of Poplar Falls, of course."

From across the lobby came a pair of men dressed in white uniforms of the care- giving staff. Both men looked at Amber as if wanting to know why they had been called.

"Could you please escort Miss Grant off the grounds?" Amber requested coldly. "And please tell Dale not to let her in again without checking with me first."

The larger of the men reached out to grasp Marci Grant's arm as he gestured towards the door. Marci shrugged off his grasp and gave him a dirty look, as if to indicate that he'd better not touch her again.

"Fine!" Marci stormed off in her red high heels. As she opened the door to her Corvette, she heard 'Soft Kitty, Warm Kitty' emanating from her purse. Once in the driver's seat, Marci dug the phone from her purse and quickly answered the call.

"Hey..." she began in a cheerful tone before being cut off.

"You're at the rehab centre, aren't you?" Trudy blurted. "Don't try and deny it."

"I'm here to see a client," Marci said. A lie, which was partly true as she did intend on trying to sell Lucy Shaffer a house in Poplar Falls; although selling her a house wasn't the only thing Marci had on her mind.

"I hate it when you lie to me," Trudy replied, muttering a curse and hanging up on her.

Marci knew Trudy would call her again later. Hopefully she would be calmer, but that was wishful thinking she realized as she drove off the Magnolia grounds.

32

Dodge sat at his desk, still running the previous night's events through his mind. After returning to the station to drop off the busted laptop, he had gone home. After his usual run, he had sat in his porch still smelling of sweat, sipping a beer, and rummaged through all the recent social media pertaining to the late Charlie Baker.

What Dodge had begun referring to as the Charlie Baker Fan Club had gained a few members, but there seemed to be a lot more hate coming out now. People had taken to referring to Charlie Baker as a gigolo, even if there was no indication that he had taken payment in any form. There was no indication anywhere that he had gotten money or gifts from the women he was seeing. Plus, not many of these women actually had money, thought Dodge. Charlie Baker was independently well to do and didn't need their money, but that didn't keep people from using the word gigolo. Dodge assumed that most who called him that didn't really know what the word meant. The words they should have used was man-whore or male slut, thought Dodge. But other than getting up to speed with what social media had to offer, the night's internet surfing had garnered no additional leads. The only thing it had led to was his clicking on a link and seeing some older porn with Charlie Baker in the starring role. Apparently word had gotten around that Charlie had made pornographic movies in the past. He regretted clicking on that link, as he could not un-see any of it. Although the link was quickly reported and removed from the social media site, a thing he was thankful for, he remembered thinking this sort of thing wouldn't help the case.

Dodge snapped back to reality as Detective Tilley entered the detective's bullpen with two coffees from Jabba-da-Java Coffee Hut. She placed one on Dodge's desk, rousing him completely from his deep thoughts about Facebook and porn.

"Find anything interesting?" Tilley asked as she cracked open her coffee and took a sip. She sat behind her desk and leaned her chair back.

"I don't know about Dodge, but I sure did," Lemkie said, startling both detectives as he spoke. They looked puzzled but said nothing as they waited for Lemkie to explain himself. He always did, although Tilley thought he had too much of a flair for the dramatic.

"Where the hell did you find that thing?" Lemkie asked.

"What?" Tilley asked, and before Dodge could speak Lemkie continued.

"Charlie Baker's laptop," Lemkie replied. "Calvin's going through the files as we speak."

Tilley looked at Dodge with a furrowed brow, which Dodge read as her being upset. Something had happened, which he hadn't shared with her, and this was disturbing.

"You didn't tell me you found Charlie Baker's laptop!" she stated before turning back to Lemkie. "You're sure it's Charlie Baker's laptop?" she asked.

"Yes, his prints were all over it. Plus, some of yours, of course," Lemkie said as he looked at Dodge. "Calvin's already hacked into it, so we know for sure."

Tilley sat upright, and her eyes lit up as she nearly choked on a sip of coffee. The realisation of what this could actually mean was setting in.

"I was worried it wouldn't even work, in the condition it was in when I found it," Dodge replied.

"It was battered to shit," Lemkie replied. "Calvin did have to fix it before he could hack it. The keyboard no longer works, and the battery was dead, but we were able to get it running...sorta. Well, Calvin got it working, so he's backing up all the files as we speak since he's worried the thing could die anytime. Plus, parts of it look to be password-protected, but that shouldn't be hard for Calvin; as long as I can pry him away from the porn," said Calvin with a smile.

"Does it have any video footage on it?" Tilley asked.

"From what we can see, yes," Lemkie replied, and he smiled again. "Calvin nearly cried when he saw how much data was on it. He's already had to watch a lot of Charlie's homemade porn from the portable hard drives and he thought he was done. With four cameras filming, I think there's a lot on it." Lemkie's smile vanished as he continued. "But what I want to know is why the laptop also has the Panty Bandit's fingerprints on it."

"What!" Tilley roughly set her cup down on her desk, spilling coffee in the process.

Dodge's expression went blank as both Lemkie and Tilley glared at him, waiting on an explanation. Dodge took a big gulp from his hot coffee and swallowed hard. He cast his eyes to the floor while reflecting on the situation at hand.

"Well?" Tilley inquired an air of annoyance.

"I'm sorry but I can't tell you where I got it just yet," Dodge said. "I need to check something out first to be sure." He got up from behind his desk. "I need you to trust me and not do anything with that just yet." He looked at both Tilley and Lemkie, then picked up his coffee and walked out of the bullpen as the dumbstruck Tilley and Lemkie merely watched, speechless.

"Just when I thought I knew that man," Lemkie said.

"You're telling me," Tilley replied.

33

Vernon locked the door to Vernon's Meats as he watched the delivery guy get back into his truck. He waved and smiled as they exchanged glances through the glass door. Vernon glanced at the large package he had left on the counter next to the cash register. He wondered what it might be as he waited for the delivery truck to drive away. Once gone and the door locked, he flipped the sign on the door that read *Back in a Flash*.

He scooped up the package, marvelling how such a big box could be so light as he headed for his office. Once there he locked the office door as if expecting someone to walk in unexpectedly, even though he was the only one there. Moving a few things out of the way, he placed the box on his desk. He looked it over, hoping the labels would tell him where the package had come from; more importantly, who sent it. He took a dull paring knife from a cup that also contained pens, which he always used as a letter opener, and with some effort cut the packing tape and opened the box, revealing packing paper. Picking out some of the paper, he grasped at a wire and pulled out a large beige lampshade. A string with a small note attached to it dangled from the shade.

I made this especially for you, the note read. The note was signed *Dave* and had an XOX below the name.

Vernon smiled briefly, then set the shade down and set to digging through the paper and finding the other half of the lamp. He pulled the lamp from the box, spilling some of the crumpled packing paper in the process. The upper half of the lamp had paper wrapped around it, which was held in place with a large blue elastic band.

The lamp was made of varnished hardwood and looked to be hand-carved, and it had an ornate wide base with a pattern carved into it. The lamp narrowed as it got taller and was covered with ornate carvings. Vernon removed the paper, revealing a wide part that had a double set of small glass LED bulbs. Under that wrapping was another note.

I thought of you when making this. Make sure it's dark and you're alone when you try it, the second note read.

Vernon peeled off the remaining wrapping and gasped. The upper part of the lamp was an intricately carved penis that Vernon recognized right away for its veins, lack of curvature, and bulbous head. He wrapped his hand around it, marvelling at how accurate it was. He set it on his desk and looked at the tall beige lampshade. He placed the lamp shade on the lamp. The metal rings clasped the top of the lamp and held firmly in place. He plugged the lamp in and flicked it on. The lamp cast a warm glow to the room. Vernon took a moment to turn off the office lights to better appreciate the glow. Then remembering how long he had been back here with nobody to serve customers, he flicked the lamp's switch to turn it off, only it didn't turn off. Instead it turned off all the bulbs except one, making the light faint. And while it made the light faint, it cast a large shadow on the wall. A shadow shaped like Dave's manhood, thought Vernon, and he became flushed as he finally understood why his lover had wanted him to be alone when he tried the lamp. Another flick of the switch turned off the lamp and Vernon left his office, to find Agatha and Geraldine waiting at the door of his shop. He smiled as he opened the door for the ladies.

"You okay, Vernon?" Geraldine asked. "You look a bit flushed."

"I'm fine," Vernon replied. "But thank you for asking. Now, what can I do for you lovely ladies on this fine day?"

Later that afternoon, Vernon would go back into his office and rearrange his desk to make room for his new lamp while disposing of the packaging. The last thing he needed was anyone asking who the lamp was from. He would tell them he got it at a craft show, he thought as he started to throw away the notes, and then had a change of heart. He would keep those. He slipped those into the last folder in his desk drawer where he kept some old newspaper clippings. His wife would never look there, he thought as he closed for the day.

34

"Have a seat," Detective Tilley said as she suddenly became self-conscious. She swivelled her chair slightly to face the chair next to her desk. She had felt fine all day but now started to feel a little underdressed in her plain blazer and dark slacks. Marci Grant dressed in a tight-fighting blazer and pants with her tattered brown driving gloves. She adjusted the chair to face Tilley as she sat down and crossed her long, shapely legs.

"You wanted to see me?" Tilley asked.

"Yes," Marci replied, but Tilley cut her off before she could continue.

"You know I can't discuss an ongoing investigation, right?" Tilley's comment had an air of disbelief about it.

"Oh, it's not about the case. Well, not exactly," the real-estate agent replied. "You see, the sale of the Turlingtons' place fell through when the Blanchards got fed up with the crime scene across the road."

"I see. But I'm not sure what it is you expect from us."

"Well, really, it's the women leaving flowers and the people constantly coming by to see who they are."

"There's nothing we can do about that," Detective Tilley replied.

"I guess I was hoping that you would be close to solving the case so you could remove the crime scene tape or something. I figure once that's no longer there, the women might stop treating it like a shrine to Charlie Baker's big Johnson. I can't see that house selling any time soon with all the commotion going on across the street."

"I understand," Tilley replied. "But there's nothing we can do for now."

"Well, it never hurts to ask," Marci said, and she smiled a little. "I'm hoping I can change the Blanchards' minds somehow. They really like the house and location but not the crime scene across the street."

"Look, I shouldn't say this, but we're working on something that could help us make progress. But I can't say more than that. I hope you understand."

"Oh I do," Marci replied as she stood up.

Tilley stood as well and marvelled at how tall Marci was as she looked up to make eye contact. Marci was a bit taller than Tilley but her heels versus the detective's flat shoes made her more so.

Marci extended a brown-gloved hand which Tilley shook awkwardly. Marci smiled, and her eyes roamed over Tilley as she spoke.

"I'd ask you to let me know when the tape will be coming down at Charlie's old place, but you probably can't do that either, can you?"

"I'm afraid not," Tilley replied as she sat behind her desk again, watching as Marci walked out of the detectives' bullpen. Tilley's phone rang, distracting her from the strange encounter she had just had. She glanced at the display on the phone and recognized the number. It was the reporter from the local paper again, probably wanting a statement still. She wondered how many times she would have to tell him that she couldn't discuss an ongoing investigation with him. She hit the ignore button on her phone, sending the call to her voicemail.

As Marci emerged from the police station, she couldn't help but notice a familiar- looking white sedan drive past. The car disappeared into traffic before Marci could confirm that this was actually Trudy's sedan. Marci knew Trudy's jealous streak was getting worse but was she following her now? Had it gotten to this point? Marci wondered as she got into her Corvette.

35

Lemkie hesitated as he entered what passed for the Crime Scene Investigator's tech lab in the police station of the small city of Poplar Falls. At a workbench used for electronics sat a clearly distraught Calvin. Calvin's expression told him something was seriously wrong.

"What's up?" Lemkie asked, to lighten the mood a bit, hoping Calvin had some good news for him.

On the counter top next to Calvin was a wired and dismantled laptop which Lemkie confirmed to be the one missing from Charlie Baker's apartment. Dodge still hadn't disclosed how he had actually acquired the busted electronic device other than he had found it near the Food Emporium. Calvin had been working on the laptop since Dodge brought it in the day before. It had been pretty damaged and the screen had died but an ever resourceful Calvin had been able to get it working again by hooking it to a monitor to start with.

Calvin cleared his throat and took a sip from a water bottle on his desk before speaking.

"It's Charlie's computer, all right. No doubt about it."

"You hacked it?"

"Yeah," Calvin replied. "I got into his file folders just now, once I got it working that is. Finally. He was either very good with computers or had a friend who is. Either way I'm in now. However, some of the file folders are still encrypted, but at least I know how to hack them now."

"What did you find?" Lemkie asked as he stood behind Calvin, placing a hand on the computer guru's shoulder and hovering. Calvin had gotten used to Lemkie expecting him to show him and not just tell him.

The monitor Calvin had wired to the laptop displayed a long list of files. Feeling Calvin's hesitation to explain, Lemkie asked his next question.

"What are those?"

"More porn," Calvin replied listlessly. He clearly wasn't happy about the find.

"A lot more?" Lemkie asked.

"Unless I'm mistaken as to how much is still encrypted, about 132 hours of it," Calvin replied. "Maybe more, I'm not sure yet."

"Oh," Lemkie said, starting to understand why Calvin had looked upset when he entered the lab. Calvin had been sorting and watching videos of Charlie ever since the case began. There were hours upon hours of porn, plus just as much footage of Charlie lying in bed chatting with his most recent conquest. Calvin now had mixed feelings about Charlie because of many of the conversations he'd had to listen to. At first, he had admired Charlie's prowess, but that turned to dislike. Calvin hadn't taken Charlie's sexual addiction (which he had been in therapy for) seriously up until he had to watch the homemade videos that Charlie was making. Although listening to a spent Charlie's conversations with the women had had an effect on Calvin. He began understanding why many of the women Charlie Baker slept with didn't hate him; even after they found out he had many lovers. Charlie was a good listener and often offered very wise advice, although that was usually only after a wild round of sex, all caught on camera, sometimes from four different angles.

Now Calvin was faced with over 132 hours of additional video footage to watch. And it would be a painful process, which was why he said he would still have to hack into many of the encrypted files. A fact which wasn't true, but he needed to buy time. He was exhausted, and the last thing he needed was pressure to go through this new batch of videos in a hurry. He already knew what to expect from the footage. With the bulk of the metadata corrupted, he couldn't know when the videos were recorded. The best he could hope for was to find something solid to go on in one of the first videos and hope to get a break from watching porn at work. It had sexually frustrated him at first, but now he found himself still addicted and yet sick of watching it. He knew this forced binging was helping him realize he had to do something about his own porn addiction. What he could do he wasn't sure, but this case wasn't helping at all.

"Good work," Lemkie said as he left the room. "Please update me if you find something important."

Calvin didn't reply. He merely sat staring at the monitor with a blank expression. A moment later he felt his stomach churn, which made him shoot out of his chair in a panic. He knew he wouldn't make it to the washroom, so he fell to his knees before a small open wastebasket full of old electronic parts and vomited into it. Once the heaving stopped, he realized that the wastebasket was made of a metal mesh and didn't have a bag to contain the whole-grain Cheerios he had just regurgitated. This realization brought on a new set of dry heaves before regaining enough strength to clean the mess he had made. He needed to clean the mess before anyone found out, as it would only give them more ammunition to make fun of him with, and he couldn't let that happen.

36

Dodge didn't like to drink caffeine after five in the afternoon, so he sipped his decaf coffee as he skimmed through the newest set of images from the busted laptop in the file on his desk. He looked over the first batch one at a time while glancing at Tilley, who was doing the same, only on her laptop computer. Calvin's having to hack each encrypted file was taking a long time, so he gave them what he had.

Tilley was still trying to get Dodge to talk about the busted laptop. Ever since Lemkie broke the news about the Panty Bandit's fingerprints being on the laptop, Dodge had been abnormally quiet. This was unlike Dodge to go quiet about a lead in a case. Especially one they figured would most likely remain unsolved unless said thief struck again. Yes, the pilfering of women's underwear had stopped, but people still felt uneasy about the fact that the Panty Bandit was still out there. Tilley knew that Dodge knew something now. It was obvious but she couldn't tell why he was being quiet about it. Was he trying to cover something up?

"You know the difference between men and women?" he asked.

"You trying to be funny?" Tilley asked as she sipped her regular coffee. Dodge may have wanted to avoid too much caffeine at this late hour but Tilley wasn't worried about it. Plus, a quick trip to the gym would take care of any extra zest left over for her.

"No, no. I mean this case about a man who slept with all these women. I mean, not all men are like that, you know."

"Are you trying to tell me all men are *not* pigs?" Tilley quipped, in an obvious tone of sarcasm. "I mean, I know Stella was in love with Charlie. She never came out and said so, but, come on."

"I hear you," Dodge replied. "And Sadie Cross, too. She said that after sex, she and Charlie would talk for hours."

"Hours?" Tilley asked.

"Hours!" Dodge replied. "She said he was an amazing listener and even gave good advice." Dodge chuckled. "After sex she said, when he wasn't a horny bastard anymore."

Tilley guffawed. She wasn't sure when Dodge had spoken with Sadie again, and between that and the Panty Bandit prints she had to wonder what else he might be hiding.

"And so this makes you say that not all men are dogs?" Tilley replied.

"Well, I meant that most men can separate sex and love."

Tilley spun her chair around and faced Dodge. She kicked her feet up on the desk nearest to her and sipped her coffee.

"Okay, so you're telling me that because a man can separate the two it doesn't make him a dog?" Tilley asked. "Help me out here, because I'm really confused," she said, smiling.

"Well, I mean that sex is lust-based; simple animalistic urges," Dodge replied. "Making love is an emotional connection and so not the same as pure sex. I mean, sexual urges are the birthplace of kink and erotica."

"What are you babbling about?" Tilley responded with a large grin as she leaned back in her chair.

Dodge put his feet up on his own desk and sipped his coffee before continuing on his late-night wisdom-filled rant.

"Well, it's true; when I was married and in love." Dodge paused and sipped coffee. "I was in love, you know. Anyway, we never had regular sex; we made love. We used to massage each other and cuddle."

Tilley's smile widened.

"I never pictured you as the soft, cuddly type," she said with a laugh.

"When you really love someone deeply, it changes you," Dodge replied in a serious tone. "But that's all behind me now. We're divorced."

"Anyway, I'm not convinced that Charlie Baker could separate love and sex," Tilley replied. "I'm not convinced he knew what love was."

"You might be right about Charlie, although Sadie seemed to think he was pretty great."

Tilley turned around and shut down her computer as she spoke.

"You're not going to tell me, are you?"

"What?"

"You mean who," Tilley replied.

"Who what?" Dodge replied, even though he knew she wanted to know what he knew about the Panty Bandit. What he suspected but had yet to confirm. Only, Dodge suddenly realised he didn't really want to know. Not anymore anyway. It would be pointless now. If he was right, it would be pointless. Although, as a detective a part of him needed the closure. But he needed some time before he would be able to tell his partner. He wanted to be sure.

"I forgot to tell you what happened this afternoon," Dodge said in an obvious attempt to change the subject.

Tilley, frustrated with Dodge's refusal to share what he knew, said nothing in reply but let him go on instead.

"That Leblanc woman I interviewed."

"The one in the old videos from the hard drive?" Tilley asked.

"Yes. I was asking her questions when she got mad at me," Dodge replied. "She got red in the face, yelled at me, and then stormed out."

"What did you say to get her so upset?"

"I asked her if she had been aware that he was seeing other women during their own affair."

"And?"

"She got mad and said, 'He never promised me a rose garden' and stormed out."

Tilley laughed, and Dodge felt the tension ease between him and the partner he was keeping in the dark.

37

Dodge was in a little earlier than usual and, while having his first morning coffee, he sat at his desk in the bullpen of the Poplar Falls police station. He sat there in sheer disbelief as he watched the surveillance camera footage from the Food Emporium on his laptop. He had heard that the video had been uploaded to YouTube almost as soon as the police officers had settled everyone down. He wondered who had done it, watching the video for the second time as he waited for Tilley. She was in the process of getting a briefing from one of the officers on the scene and she didn't know about the video yet.

The footage showed Sadie Cross, who had rounded the corner of aisle eight pushing a small but half-full shopping cart while mouthing something with an unpleasant look on her face. Dodge wished there was sound to the video as he watched a none-too- pleased Stella Rubbin carrying a partially loaded hand basket come from the aisle behind Sadie.

The women looked to be exchanging harsh words as they made their way to the checkout line. Stella seemed a little unsteady, a result of being inebriated at the time. She mouthed something to Sadie and, in reply, Sadie took a long English cucumber from Stella's basket and angrily shook it in front of the busty black woman's face. Stella staggered back a step and, in a swift motion, tried to knock the vegetable out of Sadie's grasp but only succeeded in breaking it in half instead, sending the top half flying. Sadie threw the broken cucumber at Stella, missing her intended target but grazing her cheek in the process. Stella grabbed the large bulk bag of gummy bears from her shopping basket and swung it at a flinching Sadie, who blocked it with a raised arm. The swinging bag of soft candy Stella was planning to soak in vodka burst open and its contents scattered.

The blue-haired young girl at the cash register froze in place as she watched, holding a foil-wrapped stick of butter that she was about to scan and bag. Her customer, Geraldine, the wife of Pastor George and an original member of the Naughty Knitters Club, flinched as she watched it all unfold. She flinched every time one of the women took a swing.

Geraldine grasped the blue-haired cashier's arm and spoke. The blue-haired girl then dropped the butter and grasped the phone next to her cash register. Dodge wasn't sure if she was calling 911 or the store manager. Geraldine and the cashier watched as the pair of women then began grappling with each other. The young cashier set the phone receiver down on the counter and ran around the cash register as if to try and stop the women. The young girl stopped a few feet away from the pair of women who were now rolling on a bed of gummy bears while pulling at each other's hair. The cashier touched her face where she still had a scar. She would later tell an officer the scar was of a piercing that had once been torn out in just this sort of altercation, which is why she changed her mind about getting involved.

Geraldine dug through her large purse and took out an old cell phone. She fiddled with it and then put it to her ear as she watched the store manager come running. On camera, he looked to be shouting something and began prying Sadie Cross off a subdued Stella Rubbin, who was now trying to crawl away from the smaller, usually demure little woman who sat atop her, screaming and slapping at her.

As the store manager struggled to pull the women apart, uniformed officers arrived, which seemed to take the fight out of Sadie as she allowed the manager to pull her off the crawling Stella. Stella was now scrambling away as she shoved gummy bears she had collected off the floor into her mouth as she sobbed. The manager and Sadie stumbled backward and collapsed against a rack of potato chips near the cash register, a few of the bags bursting open and scattering potato chips with the gummy bears.

When the video clip ended, Geraldine was on the phone frantically talking to someone as the blue-haired cashier's arms were flailing about while she spoke to the manager, most likely explaining what had transpired. Each uniformed officer was tending to the women who, moments before, had been locked in battle over what Dodge assumed was the late Charlie Baker. The YouTube clip went to grey and ended just as Tilley arrived. Before she could utter a single word, an excited Dodge spoke as he hit play on the video again.

"You have *got* to see this," he said enthusiastically.

38

"Rumour is, Vernon Cross is gay," Myrtle said as she wriggled in her cushy chair to get comfortable. She was knitting on the same deep purple scarf she had worked on during their last few meetings. The scarf was now over four feet long and getting longer still.

"Who?" Ester asked. She sat across from Myrtle in a La-Z-Boy, knitting a deformed sweater.

In a last-minute debate, the ladies of the Naughty Knitters Club had decided to hold their meeting in a room ordinarily reserved for reading and other such quiet activities at the Magnolia Wellness Centre. The plush furniture was Ester's idea, as those old padded wooden chairs in the meeting room always made her artificial hip ache and put her butt to sleep.

"You know, the owner of the meat market," Geraldine said, while knitting squares for a blanket for one of her grandchildren.

"He's married to that Sadie Cross woman," Emma added as she unravelled some yarn. "She's a suspect in the Charlie Baker murder investigation, you know."

"Oh, shush," Mavis said. "Ever since those detectives gave you their cards, you think you're Agatha Christie or something."

"Or that writer lady who solved murders," Myrtle added with a smile and a wink. "That *Murphy Brown* lady."

"You idiot," Agatha groused. "You mean Jessica Fletcher. That *Murder She Wrote* woman who saw more death than the Grim Reaper."

"I love that show," Myrtle blurted.

"Who?" Ester asked?

"Well, she was sleeping with Charlie Baker," Emma said. "I know, I seen her car there many times."

"That doesn't mean she killed him," Geraldine said. "Just

means she was horny, and if Vernon is gay he probably wasn't giving her any."

"I never said she did it," Emma said with a smile. "I just said she's a suspect."

"Well," Myrtle added, "whether she did it or not doesn't change the fact that people are saying Vernon is gay."

"I heard it, too," Agatha said with a smile. "I heard he really loves his sausages."

Laughter erupted in the room as the ladies busied themselves with their knitting.

"Those are just rumours," Geraldine said. "Although I'm told someone saw him going into a motel with some guy."

"I heard he was caught in his car on a back road on the outskirts of town," Agatha added.

"Who cares what he puts in his mouth," Myrtle said. "Did you ladies hear about all the videos Charlie had? Home movies of him having sex."

"Get out!" Mavis exclaimed as she set down her knitting to pay attention.

"Who?" Ester asked.

Emma set down her knitting and got up and walked over to Ester. She turned up the volume on Ester's hearing aid, knowing full well the batteries were weak again.

"Thank you," Geraldine said as she rolled her eyes.

"What videos?" Emma asked. "Nobody told me anything about videos."

"Rumour is that ever since the murder, Calvin Crawford has been watching videos of Charlie Baker having sex," Myrtle said. She smiled and looked around to see reactions to this juicy bit of gossip she had been saving up for this meeting.

"Get out!" Mavis exclaimed, flushing with jealousy at the idea that Myrtle would have the juiciest gossip of the evening.

"Having sex with who?" Ester asked.

"Everyone, from what I hear," Myrtle said as she tried to suppress her glee.

"That can't be true. Not in my apartment building," Agatha stated as her face flushed. She hid what she knew well. A feeling of panic arose in her about the peephole. Would word get out? She couldn't help but wonder. Would gossip spread more than it already had? Surely her friends would tell her. Of course they would, and they would tease her endlessly.

Emma laughed at Agatha's sudden discomfort, knowing full well she must have known since she lived in the apartment next to Charlie Baker's.

"They say they found cameras everywhere," Myrtle added, who had stopped knitting as she spoke. "I heard that's why Sadie and that Stella woman were fighting at the grocery store."

Agatha swallowed hard and felt her anxiety level rise. She felt a panic attack coming on but managed to suppress it.

"Oh, don't get me started on that again," Geraldine blurted, who was more than glad to talk about the altercation at the Food Emporium, although she pretended she didn't want to. She often put up this act, as being the wife of a pastor she had to at least pretend to be a respectable lady; a respectable lady who takes part in a group therapy session for sexual addiction with other ladies who happen to knit while in session. Knit and gossip.

"Gummy bears everywhere," Geraldine said. "I thought I was going to die. Those women are bat-shit crazy, I tell you."

"Never mind that," Mavis said, looking at Myrtle. "I wanna hear more about those videos."

"I'm hoping they end up on the internet," Myrtle said as her face flushed. "I'd love to see those."

"I bet you would," Emma replied, laughing at her own comment. "Rumour is that comedian Lucy Shaffer is one of the women in them."

Agatha and Mavis gasped simultaneously at that comment.

"Are we ever going to do any therapy tonight?" Myrtle asked with a pout as she knitted furiously.

"You just want to brag about one of your booty calls," Ester said with a smile.

"Oh, shush," Emma replied. "I wanna hear this one. Was it that young one you mentioned last time? The one with the big lump in his crotch who liked older women?"

39

Calvin sat at his desk in the tech lab, a can of Red Bull sitting next to a prescription bottle of anxiety medication. He was starting to dread coming into work and barely sleeping at night. He had never been this sexually frustrated in his life, and the worst part about it was that everybody knew it. Being a porn addict he had thought it amazing at first to get to watch some of it on the job, but that quickly lost its appeal. At home, he had his favourite websites and all the privacy in the world. The stress of it all was getting to him, but he couldn't let anyone know, as they would never let him live it down. The merciless teasing was already rampant and knowing the effect it was having would only make it worse.

Today, waiting for him on his desk was a large can of Red Bull, an open box of tissues, lube, and the evidence bag of Viagra. The energy drink he had cracked open right away and took a large gulp before even sitting down at his desk. The clear plastic bag containing the Viagra and the other items he pushed aside. He'd put that away later, he thought as he adjusted his man parts, noticing how sore his masturbating arm was. He opened the side drawer on his desk and pulled out a brochure while he looked about in paranoia to be sure nobody would see him. He unfolded it, revealing a serene-looking landscape with black print over it.

Magnolia Wellness and Rehabilitation Centre

Are addictions holding you back, hurting those you love and affecting your career? Do you suffer from an addiction to drugs, alcohol, or sex? The dedicated and highly-trained staff at the Magnolia Wellness and Rehabilitation Centre are here to help you get your life back on track.

Our services include counselling with licensed therapists and access to amazing support groups. All of this is provided while staying at the serene and relaxing Magnolia estate, which is nestled on the outskirts of the small and beautiful city of Poplar Falls, filled with small-town charm and surrounded by the relaxing splendor of rivers and picturesque waterfalls.
Come stay a while and let us help you.

Stella P. Rubbin
Magnolia Wellness and Rehabilitation Centre Manager

He needed help and he knew it. His porn addiction had been manageable in the past but now he felt it spinning out of control. He would need to check their website, but he didn't dare do it while at work. He couldn't risk anyone finding out if he wanted to continue working in Poplar Falls.

Hearing the door to the lab open, he quickly put the brochure back where he had gotten it and swept the pill bottle into the drawer as well, slamming it shut harder than he would have liked. He turned to see Lemkie, who clearly had no reason to be in the lab but was pretending he did, so he could check on Calvin and the gag items they'd placed on his desk.

"What?" Calvin barked.

"Captain was just asking if we had any information.

Any leads. Apparently, he says Dodge and Tilley are busy interviewing women, so he asked me to check into it." Even though he tried to make this sound convincing, Calvin knew this was horse shit. The look on Lemkie's face said so.

"Tell the captain I'm working on it and that he's welcome to help if he really wants to."

"Naw, I'm pretty sure it's okay," Lemkie replied with a grin.

"I thought so."

"Some of the officers and I are going to lunch later; they said to ask if you wanted to join us. You in?" Lemkie asked.

"No thanks," Calvin replied, who knew this would end up with them poking fun at his task at hand. "I'm not hungry. Plus, I've got a lot of work to do."

"Living the dream, huh?" Lemkie asked, in a half-question, half-comment tone.

"Are you serious?" Calvin asked. "What does that even mean? Living what dream? Whose dream is this? TELL ME. I want to know."

Lemkie picked up a stapler from a table, pretending he needed it and spun around, heading back the way he had come in.

"Wait... what dream? Whose dream? What the..." Calvin exclaimed. He didn't have to finish what he was saying, as Lemkie had left the room. Probably telling everyone about him getting upset, he thought. That's when his stomach churned and he remembered being told to take the pills with food. He barely had time to spin his chair away from his desk, hoping to find an empty evidence bag nearby, but vomiting on the floor instead. Thoughts of the dozens of videos still left to watch made his stomach churn.

A sound of incoming email had Calvin mousing his way to his inbox to see an email from Tilley.

"Any news on those vids yet?" the email read.

Calvin's stomach lurched and he vomited yet again.

40

Dodge parked his rusty Ford Escape in the parking lot of Elder's Funeral Parlor and took his fresh hot coffee from the cup holder. Detective Tilley sat in the passenger seat, holding her own coffee cup by its rims to avoid burning her fingers. With the windows down, parked facing the street, both detectives sat quietly sipping out of cardboard cups bearing the Jabba-da-Java Coffee Hut logo. Dodge had asked Tilley to get out of the office for coffee so they could brainstorm. But Tilley had gotten to know her partner fairly well and so she felt something was off. She didn't know him well enough to know what, just that something was off with him. Dodge sipped his coffee and finally broke the silence.

"You know, romance is dead," Dodge said. "With today's age of porn, erotica, hook-up websites, etc., romance is dead."

"Is there booze in that cup?" Tilley asked jokingly. "Bailey's in your coffee?"

"I mean, men think its okay to text pictures of their dicks to women," Dodge replied, ignoring Tilley's joke. "Somehow men think this is okay and that it will actually turn a woman on."

Tilley smiled as she sipped her coffee. She had been thinking about Stella's trip to the morgue. Normal people don't do such a thing. Stella was still obsessing about Charlie Baker, long after he was found murdered. Plus, she had started drinking again. Tilley was tempted to bet on Stella being the killer, but she couldn't do such a thing. A wager on a case like this could have serious repercussions if word ever got out. She had tried to tell her fellow officers that pools like this shouldn't happen, but she suspected many of the patrolmen already had one going. The captain would lose it if he found out.

"I'm sure there are still plenty of romantic men out there," Tilley replied.

"Some," Dodge replied, "sure, but not many."

"Have you ever?" Tilley asked.

"What?" Dodge asked.

"Texted a woman a picture of your junk?"

"Hell no!" Dodge exclaimed in disbelief. "I can't believe you had to ask."

Tilley smiled as she sipped the coffee. Soon they were sitting in an awkward silence again. Dodge eventually straightened himself in his seat as he adjusted his rear-view mirror.

"Remember when you asked me about the fingerprints on the laptop?" Dodge asked as he shot a glance at Tilley and then back to the rear-view mirror.

"The Panty Bandit's fingerprints? How could I forget about that?"

"I know why he stopped breaking into houses and stealing women's underwear," Dodge replied.

Before Tilley could reply, Dodge pointed to the passenger side of the vehicle. Tilley turned to watch as Walter pedaled his tricycle and wagon past them, hauling his usual load of recyclables. Walter's pants looked three sizes too big and appeared to not have been washed in who knows how long. The pants were held up by an old belt which looked to be cinched tight. Walter looked their way as he pedaled past the truck and smiled his best, scruffy-looking smile. His teeth were yellow and he looked like he hadn't shaved in a while, although Walter couldn't have grown a beard if his life depended on it.

"Wednesday," Walter said as he biked past them. "Wednesday," he repeated as he turned his tricycle into the street and went on his way.

"Holy crap," Tilley whispered.

"I know," Dodge replied.

If Walter really was the Panty Bandit then his days of stealing women's underwear had to be over, thought Tilley.

Or would they be? She glanced at her partner and then back at the frail-looking young man pedaling away. The first phase of learning an unbelievable truth was denial; a refusal to accept it as fact. Walter had been a quiet young man before the tumour. Not the smartest of kids and very dedicated to his mother, the only real family he had in this city. Her disability pension meant they struggled, but Walter had been a dedicated son. Tilley couldn't fathom how it was possible for this young man to have been the Panty Bandit all this time. Of course, those days were over, she thought. Or was this Dodge pulling her leg?

"Are you serious?" Tilley asked. "Or are you messing with me?"

"I sure do wish he could still talk," Dodge replied. "I saw his tricycle outside the Food Emporium, and right there in the front basket was the laptop. I'd love to know where he got it."

"He gave it to you?"

"I took it while he was still inside," Dodge replied.

"Did he see you?"

"I don't think so," Dodge replied as he sipped his coffee. He glanced at Tilley, trying to read her expression to see how she felt about all this. She looked to be filled with confusion and disbelief. He knew she would have trouble with this, which is one reason he hadn't told her right away. The other reason was that he simply took the laptop from Walter's tricycle and wasn't sure if anyone had seen him. It would most likely be on the Food Emporium's surveillance camera footage. And then there was Walter. Simple Walter, whose vocabulary now consisted mostly of the days of the week. Brain damage was a bitch, thought Dodge. But, then again, was she? When you thought about it, Walter wasn't an innocent young man after all. Perhaps this was poetic justice for his crimes. Okay, he had never committed any sexual assault, but he instilled fear in a good part of the community.

Especially the women of Poplar Falls. And knowing that his motor skills were now impaired meant those days were over, thought Dodge. But the community didn't know this, and most people assumed the Panty Bandit would strike again someday. Most people believed it was only a matter of time.

"I watched him leave after I took it," Dodge said. "He looked like he forgot it was there in the first place."

"Did anyone see you?" Tilley asked.

"Not that I know of," Dodge replied. "Although I was a little worried after watching the brawl at the Food Emporium on YouTube. I figured if someone watched the security footage they might have seen me taking it."

"True," Tilley replied.

"I've been keeping an eye on Walter since Lemkie found his prints on the laptop," Dodge replied. "I wanted to go talk to his mother, but I'm not sure how to go about it without making her ask why."

"You're assuming she doesn't already know," his partner replied, in true Detective Tilley fashion. "Some mothers are all-seeing." Tilley thought of her own mother as she said this.

Dodge shot his partner a glance that told Tilley he had not considered this as a possibility.

"You think he would ever do it again?" Tilley asked.

"I doubt it," Dodge replied. "He can barely function now and can hardly speak, so, how could he?"

"Have you told anyone?"

"Just you," Dodge replied. "I mean, I want to, but what will that accomplish?"

"It would close the case, for one thing," Tilley replied as she finished her coffee but kept the cup to busy her hands. "And stop women from wondering if the Panty Bandit will strike again."

"Well, I don't know about you, but I can't see that happening."

"It would also keep women from suspecting innocent

men," Tilley replied. "Did you think about that?"

"Actually, I never did think of it that way," Dodge replied as he drank the last of his coffee.

"You wouldn't," Tilley replied. "Men can forget this type of thing but women can't."

"You think all men are pigs, don't you?" Dodge asked.

"Not all men," Tilley replied with a smile. "But most of them are. But I hope you don't think women are that much better," she added with a smile.

Dodge started his rusty Ford Escape and pulled out of the parking lot and headed towards the local bottle depot, where he assumed Walter would be going at this hour.

"I need you to help me figure out this Panty Bandit thing," Dodge said.

Tilley was starting to understand why Dodge hadn't told anyone where he had found Charlie Baker's old laptop. She also understood why he hadn't said anything about the Panty Bandit's prints either. If word got out, someone might hurt Walter. Although a small part of her thought he might deserve it, another part of her wondered if he even remembered that part of his past. Walter was very different since the life-altering surgery that saved his life.

They watched Walter go to the recycling depot and drop off his cargo. They waited until he left and followed him home. Walter was oblivious to the pair of detectives following him. And even if he had seen them, he wouldn't have known they were actually following him and why. Walter had a one-track mind now and pedaling his tricycle with a destination in mind was hard work for him.

41

His tricycle and wagon tucked away, Walter stood before the large freezer in his trailer, digging through his pockets to find today's earnings. He would need to put this with the rest; in the box that contained coins and bills sitting on top of a red silk garment lining the bottom of the cardboard box. This red silk pair of panties, which he had stolen from one of his last outings before his surgery, never made it to his hiding place with the rest; a hiding place that his mother had found in the back of his bedroom closet. Walter always waited until his mother was asleep before digging out the boxes and obsessing over his collection. Walter's tricycle used to belong to his mother when she was still able to make it to the grocery store herself. But eventually Walter had to take that over and this gave him freedom. Freedom to roam was the reason he had stolen his first pair of panties, taking them from a clothesline while no one was looking. He had been irresistibly drawn to the silky underwear, his very first theft. The adrenaline of stealing them added to the rush he got from possessing them. He fondled them nightly for a month before the excitement began to wane. The thrill of the theft began plaguing his mind, more than the underwear itself. Soon, he would steal another pair from a clothesline, but the excitement he felt from this one wouldn't last a week. He began obsessing over the idea of stealing dirty women's underwear. He grew excited at the mere thought of it. Before his operation Walter wasn't the smartest, but he could be calculating. He picked the location of his first break-in by figuring out her routine. His first victim, the newly-divorced Mrs. Weatherbee, had a routine that wasn't hard to figure out. Laundry day was always Tuesday nights and so Mondays, when she would be at school teaching, her place would be empty and her underwear dirty. Unbeknownst to Mrs. Weatherbee, she would be Walter's first victim.

He had entered the house through a back window that had been left open, so there was nothing broken. His fear of getting caught had overridden his perverted urges, and so he had taken the very first pair of red silk panties at the top of the hamper and left. Mrs. Weatherbee only noticed her red underwear was missing about a week later and assumed it probably had gone the way of the legendary missing socks her ex-husband always used to talk about. She would never know she had been the very first victim in what would become a rash of break-and-enters.

Walter would take the tricycle out, riding through the same neighbourhoods he now collected his recyclables in. Wanting to steal dirty underwear, he would need to know when laundry day was; that was easy enough for his then-sharper mind. Clotheslines were obvious, but not everyone used those. But Walter could smell the fabric softener wafting from the dryer vents as he biked past the houses that were doing laundry, and many were sticklers for routine which meant laundry day was always the same day of the week. Mrs. Weatherbee was Tuesdays and her neighbour, who Walter didn't know, was Sundays. And Friday nights were date night for the couple, which often meant their house would be empty for hours. They would be the first to report a break-in but it would take a while before they realized what had been taken. After the fourth break-in, people realized what was being stolen and the thief was quickly branded the Panty Bandit. Mrs. Weatherbee always remained oblivious to having been his first victim.

Now Walter's stash, which had been his prized possession, was growing mouldy. Walter hadn't been in the back of his closet since part of his mind had been carved out and thrown away like trash. It was as if they had cut out the part of him that had gotten sexually aroused by women's panties. Reality was that Walter hadn't had a sexual thought since the life-saving procedure. The procedure that had saved his life and had changed him forever had also stopped his criminal behaviour. Something his mother had figured out, but she never saw the point of reminding Walter of this fact.

But now, simple-minded Walter added today's earnings

into the same cardboard box he had been putting all his money into since he'd started collecting recyclables. He thought about counting it but was afraid he would end up frustrated like the last time.

Walter took a folded and crumpled paper from his back pocket and looked at it for a long moment. A single tear flowed down his dirty cheek, cleaning a path down to his chin in the process. Walter tossed the paper onto the pile of random papers which cluttered the top of the old freezer. Crumpled as it was, it blended in with the rest of the tattered papers. Walter's stomach growled, and his one-track mind was refocusing on the task at hand, which would be to crack open a can of food and eat. The old electric can opener which used to make a lot of abnormal noises no longer worked, so he turned to his manual one. He pried it open to get at the food inside. As he spooned the cold food into his hungry mouth, again he looked longingly at the microwave with the blackened side vent. Walter had forgotten that cans are not supposed to go into the microwave. His mother had told him this, but being simple wasn't easy. But right now Walter only cared about one thing and that was eating his large can of cold stew. And sleep. Walter was always tired, but dehydration would have that effect on anyone.

42

Calvin sat at a desk next to a uniformed officer while giving a statement as Detectives Dodge and Tilley entered the bullpen at the Poplar Falls Police Station. Next to the officer sat Lemkie, who was smiling a little too much. Only later would they think that odd, since he was Calvin's boss. Calvin's left eye was puffed up and blackened as he spoke to the officer.

"What the hell happened to you?" Tilley asked.

"Long story," Calvin replied.

"Spill it. You and Lemkie disagree on which is best, *Star Trek* or *Star Wars*?" Dodge joked.

"Very funny," Lemkie replied with a frown. "Everyone knows it's *Star Trek*," which got him a dirty look from Calvin, who preferred *Star Wars*.

"I was leaving for work this morning and some guy jumps me," Calvin said. His gaze went back and forth between Dodge and Tilley, waiting to see when they would lose their cool and laugh.

"You got mugged outside your apartment?" Tilley asked. "Agatha's not going to like that." Calvin lived in one of Agatha's many apartments.

"Not mugged," the officer replied, who looked at Lemkie before letting Calvin continue telling his story.

"Well, I thought he wanted money. I would have given it to him, too," Calvin added. "He wanted a list of names of the women on the sex tapes."

"What?" Detective Tilley exclaimed.

Dodge's brow furrowed as he spoke. "How did he know about the porn?"

All of them looked at Dodge with sarcasm in their eyes, but none of them spoke aloud the fact that rumours were rampant all over Poplar Falls.

"Did you see who it was?" Tilley asked.

"A white guy, but he was wearing a ski mask," Calvin replied. "I figure he had to be at least in his forties. I mean, he called them sex tapes and not videos."

"What did you tell him?" Dodge asked.

"Nothing, which is why he gave me this," Calvin said, pointing to his blackened left eye.

"Living the dream," Lemkie said as he got up to leave, knowing full well the response he would get from his frustrated employee.

"What the fuck does that mean?" Calvin shouted after

Lemkie. "No, tell me!"

43

After a full day of interviewing many of Charlie Baker's past lovers Dodge sat in his screened porch, still in his running shorts and t-shirt, nursing a cold beer and sitting with his laptop as usual after a run. Tilley, arriving from her trip to the gym, came straight over.

"Anything interesting on Facebook tonight?" she asked as she entered the porch and perched herself on the ledge of the screened-in window.

"I'm surprised you didn't already hear," Dodge replied. He gestured for Tilley to help herself to a beer.

"What now?" She shook her head no to the offer of a beer.

"I just got off the phone with Lemkie and he thinks they got hacked."

"What hack? When?"

Dodge set his beer down, clicked at the laptop for a moment, and then turned it to show his partner. On the screen was a still of a naked blonde woman on her hands and knees. Charlie Baker was kneeling behind her, giving her everything he had, which turned out to be a lot if the look on the blonde's face was anything to go by, thought Tilley.

"Is that—" Tilley asked.

"Lucy Shaffer," Dodge replied.

"Lemkie says Calvin is convinced someone hacked into his computer. Although, from what they can tell, the only footage they've found online is the Lucy Shaffer footage."

"Well, it does make sense since she's a celebrity and all. Although I'm not sure if I want to know how you found out about the video being posted on some porn site."

Dodge laughed as he clicked away at his laptop and

showed a tabloid magazine website's front page to Tilley.

"Google search," Dodge stated. "It's where you tell Google to flag you of stuff that pops up online using the key word you wanted to watch for."

"Whoa... look at you," Tilley quipped. "Since when did you get to be Mr. Tech Savvy?"

Dodge gave her a look indicating that, while he preferred the old paper methods, he wasn't completely inept when it came to computers.

"Anyway, our friend Charlie Baker has been trending since this afternoon when the tabloid posted an article about the porn site's video with him and Lucy Shaffer."

"You should set up one of those things for Lucy Shaffer," Tilley replied.

"I already did," Dodge replied. "Rumour is her agent is suing the porn site but I'm betting it's a publicity stunt."

"How is a video of her having sex publicity?" Tilley asked.

"I'm just waiting to see if any other videos of Charlie end up online as well," Dodge replied as he sipped his beer.

"You disappointed that Calvin hasn't found any vids of Charlie Baker with Ms. Weatherbee?"

"Well, I do admit I was sort of surprised there were none," Dodge replied.

"Not me. Although I was shocked to see her at his door that morning," Tilley replied. "I did tell you that I bumped into her at the grocery store, didn't I?"

"Not that I recall," Dodge replied curiously. He found it odd for Tilley to have withheld this information from him.

The truth of the matter was that once Tilley had caught Marci staring at her so intensely, she had forgotten all about her conversation with Ms. Weatherbee.

"She wanted me to tell you she's no whore," Tilley said with a smile.

"Noted," Dodge replied, focusing his attention on his

laptop. He didn't look up in that moment, but Tilley could tell he was paying attention. It was obvious to her that he had been curious about Ms. Weatherbee ever since he had laid eyes on her curvaceous body.

"Well, let me know if you find out anything else," Tilley said as she made her way to the door.

"I will," Dodge replied as he watched her leave. Once he saw her cross the street, he minimized the Facebook page and went back to the porn site and hit play on the video of Lucy Shaffer and Charlie Baker getting it on. And while it wasn't graphic porn with close-ups and all, the footage hadn't been edited and was all from one single camera angle. Dodge knew instantly why the video had gone viral so quickly. Lucy was a very attractive woman and Charlie was really giving what had to be the performance of his life. Although Dodge hadn't watched much of the homemade porn, so he didn't really have much of a comparison. He made a mental note to ask Lemkie about that in the morning. Calvin would just love discussing porn with the detectives, thought a grinning Dodge. But sadly Lemkie would have to do.

During their telephone call, Lemkie had explained that Calvin said he was finished hacking all the files and so had access to all the videos now. But Calvin was also in the process of what Dodge liked to call a burnout. Calvin gave Lemkie a note from his doctor saying he needed a few days away from digging through pornography all day. None of them knew that Calvin was a porn addict, but he normally didn't watch porn at work. But since he got attacked, his stress levels had peaked and he needed time off. Lemkie might have expressed this had Calvin not vomited on his shoes moments after giving him his doctor's note. Lemkie's new expensive sneakers with the fancy laces would smell of Calvin's nervous stomach content for a week.

44

Vernon thought it strange when he pulled into his driveway to see his elegant two-storey house completely dark. It wasn't strange for him to work late, as he did it all the time. Owning a business is a lot of work. Something both he and his wife knew very well since they each had businesses of their own. But it was strange that the hall lights weren't on like they always were when he ran late. The outside sensor light came on as soon as he opened the car door, illuminating the immaculate landscaping and stone walkway leading to the house. He gathered a pair of grocery bags from the car and paused, looking up at the second-floor window as if wanting to make sure he had not imagined the lights being off. He checked his digital watch which he gotten as a Christmas present from his wife a few years before. It read 11:45 PM. His rendezvous with Dave had made him much later than he had expected it to. Mind you, he had no regret about agreeing to meet on such short notice. Dave had made it worth the time and then some, thought Vernon as he walked up the walkway, smiling absentmindedly.

Once inside, Vernon set his keys on the entry table and kicked off his shoes. Noticing a faint glow emanating from the living room, he peered in to see the television playing a Tom Hanks and Meg Ryan movie. The sound of the television was barely audible as Hanks and Ryan were having a conversation in what looked like a library or maybe a bookstore.

On the couch lay his wife, her arms wrapped up in the pillow under her head, a spot of drool under her chin. On the coffee table before her sat a half-empty bottle of white wine, a near-empty wine glass, and three-quarters of a large slab of dark chocolate. Next to all that was a copy of the local newspaper, folded so that the picture of the flowers at Charlie Baker's place was showing. Vernon took the grocery bags to the kitchen, putting them away before going back into the living room.

He glanced at his watch again and decided that waking his wife would most likely mean having to explain the hour at which he had come home to find her sleeping on the couch. Instead he took the fuzzy blanket off the back of the couch and gently laid it over the woman he married; his high school sweetheart, whom he still loved very much. Only now he wasn't as confused as he had been in his teenage years. He knew now that he was gay, no doubt about it anymore. But the problem was, he still loved his wife more than ever and couldn't bear the idea of hurting her, so telling her was out of the question. He knew she was sexually frustrated and that's why she had slept with that damned Charlie Baker. A fact that pissed him off at first, but he quickly got over it as he wasn't exactly taking care of her needs in the sex department. Nor did he have any interest of rekindling this part of his marriage either. He was more than fine with their sex life being nonexistent at this point, especially since he had met Dave. Vernon had had a few male lovers over the years but none of them were relationship material. But Dave he thought about a lot and could see himself being with him. But the thought of telling his wife brought a tear to his eye. A tear he wiped away as he turned off the television and made his way upstairs. The bed would feel empty without his wife in it but it would be easier than explaining why he had come home so late.

45

Sadie opened an eye just enough to watch her husband walk out of the living room. His gently covering her with the blanket had awoken her but she hadn't budged. She knew it was probably very late but was too tired to have the conversation about why her husband was only getting home at this hour. Also, a part of her was jealous. She had smelled the sex on him and that saddened her. Her husband, her high school sweetheart, was getting some but she wasn't. Not anymore. Not since Charlie Baker was murdered. Lord knew her Vernon hadn't touched her in years and she knew he had no interest in ever doing so again. But she had been chilled and the blanket was so warm. It was obvious that he still loved her but not like a husband should love a wife. He never kissed her anymore and she longed for that. To be touched, caressed, kissed, and made love to. A tear rolled down her cheek and onto the pillow. As she heard the floor upstairs creak slightly as Vernon tried to be quiet, her mind wandered to the hours spent at Charlie's place. She reached out an arm towards the giant slab of dark chocolate on the coffee table but felt too drained to move anything else, so she let her arm drop lifelessly down the side of the couch.

Her thoughts now of Charlie Baker, she smiled gently and closed her eyes. He was a great lover, yes, but he always held her afterwards and before he came along, she had not had that in years. They would often talk for hours after, before making love for a second time. Charlie got a lot of help from pharmaceuticals but it didn't matter to Sadie. It was the perfect arrangement for her, as they were both getting what they wanted. Charlie wanted sex and she wanted intimacy. Falling in love with Charlie Baker was never part of the plan. It just happened. Sure, he wasn't relationship material and she knew it. He was a womanizer and a sex addict who had ruined all his previous relationships. She knew because he had told her all about it. Charlie told her how his girlfriend caught him cheating and left him. He told her all about losing custody of his daughter. Charlie wasn't afraid of opening up. He was deathly afraid of commitment but not of intimacy. Sadie fell in love with how Charlie Baker made her feel. Now that was gone, she thought. A fresh tear rolled down her cheek and onto her pillow as she drifted off to sleep.

46

An hour later, roused from a dream, Sadie sat up on the couch, covered in a cold sweat. She felt confused, flushed, and out of breath. Convinced the dream had been real, she felt her face with the back of her fingers and it was warm to the touch. She swung her legs off the couch, sat up, and looked at her surroundings. She sat in her own dark living room which confirmed it was only a dream; a very vivid dream, but a dream nonetheless. Sitting in the dark, she realized that she was sexually aroused. She reached for her dark chocolate, took a bite, and leaned back on the couch. She closed her eyes and thought about the dream in which her husband was making love to her while Charlie shouted directions and watched. In the dream, she and Vernon had paused in their lovemaking to look at Charlie Baker for his approval. Charlie had held up a score card which read 5.2 as he shouted words of encouragement at Vernon. Sadie woke just as Charlie had shoved Vernon off her and was telling Vernon to watch carefully, as he would show him how to please his frustrated wife.

Now, alone on the couch, Sadie took another bite of her dark chocolate, tossed the rest onto the coffee table, and leaned back and began touching herself through the pants she was still wearing. But now, in her fantasy, Vernon was watching as Charlie made mad, passionate love to her.

Vernon would find his wife still sleeping on the couch the next morning, naked under the blanket, with a smear of dark chocolate on her cheek and drool on her pillow.

47

Agatha sat at her kitchen table with Ester and Myrtle flanking her. Before her on the table was her new laptop, in the process of booting up for the very first time.

"I'm going to show you the best sites," Myrtle said with a smile.

"I just want to see the one of Charlie and that Shaffer woman in my apartment," Agatha replied as she impatiently waited for the computer to finish.

"Boy, did that young kid at the store blush when I asked him if he could get good porn on the computer," Ester said. She laughed and her dentures almost popped out in the process.

"I knew we shouldn't have brought you along," Agatha replied as she blushed. "You said that on purpose to embarrass me. And you," Agatha said to Myrtle. "You were almost raping him with your eyes."

"He was handsome," Myrtle said as the computer came on.

A frustrated Agatha unsuccessfully fiddled with the laptop computer and the wireless mouse, only to let Myrtle take it over to set it up.

"Why did I let you talk me into buying this damned thing?" Agatha remarked impatiently.

Myrtle turned the laptop slightly to face her as she set up shortcut icons on the desktop. She set up a web browser, explaining the basics of what the kids call surfing the internet. Agatha felt overwhelmed; learning to set her VCR had been a challenge back in the day. A few moments later Myrtle had most of what she wanted set up, with only one thing left to do.

"Okay, so what do you want to use as a Wi-fi password?" Myrtle asked as she looked at Agatha.

"A what?" Agatha replied.

"What's a why fry?" Ester asked.

"It's a password," Myrtle replied. "Here," she said as she typed and clicked away on the laptop while Agatha and Ester tried to keep up.

"Should I write this down? I probably won't remember

this password you're talking about."

"Oh, you will," Myrtle replied. "Your Wi-fi password is Big Sweaty Balls," Myrtle added, while Ester burst into laughter.

"Oh, you," Agatha replied before cracking up herself. Embarrassment aside, she had to admit it was pretty funny.

A few minutes later, Agatha sat speechless as Myrtle navigated a pornographic website. Ester sat motionless, uttering many an *Oh, my* and adding more than one *Holy Mary Mother of Jesus.*

48

"There's a cop here to see you," the young woman at the reception desk said to Stella as she walked past the front lobby of the Magnolia Wellness and Rehabilitation Centre.

Stella, who was back to work after completing part of her own rehab at the centre, was a recovering alcoholic. She found that working helped keep her mind off things that would make her want to drink again. Six years Stella had remained sober. A fact she had been very proud of and would often tell people, her way of reminding herself that she was on the right track. She also loved helping others find their own path. Stella loved what she did now even if she ran the accommodations side of the business and not the rehab side. And she might have never fallen off the proverbial wagon if the centre was for alcoholics only. But, alas, it was not. They also treated sex addicts and Stella didn't have a sex addiction. But she was a red-blooded mature woman with needs and desires just like everybody else. And even if she had a few short-lived relationships over the years, Stella had managed to stay out of trouble as the manager of the centre. She avoided trouble fairly easily until Charlie Baker arrived at the centre for treatment of his sex addiction. In their very first meeting Charlie's eyes wandered over her, which made her uncomfortable at first. She attributed it to his inability to make eye contact but when he kept staring at her bosom, she knew he would be a challenge for the centre. But the real problem was that Charlie Baker would turn out to be very charming.

Stella justified her first sexual encounter with Charlie by repeating something Emma O'Brien had told her many times: *We're not trying to tell people to never have sex again. We're merely trying to help them get control over their desires, so their lust doesn't rule their everyday lives.* Stella thought that Emma was very wise and so figured that having sex with Charlie Baker that first time, in a linen closet, would be perfectly fine. This is what she had told herself. The second time, a week later, she wasn't so sure. She did think that he needed an outlet and had noticed him flirting with a lot of women at the centre. But their conversations were so engaging and he so charming. He made her laugh, and she would catch him staring at her bouncing bosom. At first she was put off by this. Annoyed, she quickly got over it and it made her feel desirable again. Something she hadn't felt in a long time. Alcoholism has a way of taking center stage in one's life. But soon she found herself wearing low-cut tops at work and seeking Charlie out so she could flirt with him. It wasn't long before they ended up at Charlie Baker's new apartment in town, where Stella would have some of the best sex she had ever had; mostly because Charlie had a way of stimulating her mind as well as her body. Sure, she'd had great lovers in her life but there was something about Charlie Baker that made the sex so much better. And the long chats afterwards were the reason Stella came back, many times.

"Do you have time to see him?" the young woman asked, snapping Stella out of the daze she had been in all that morning. "Do you have time to meet with this cop? He asked for the owner, but I told him she wasn't in and that I would get the manager."

"Yeah, sure," Stella replied. "I'll see him."

Stella couldn't help but wonder what the cops wanted from her now. Ever since the incident at the morgue, she had spilled her guts and they knew there was nothing more to the story. They had to know. She hadn't called it love, but they knew she wasn't the killer. She couldn't be. She missed Charlie too much to have done something to end what they had, she thought. But there were rumours of the videos Charlie Baker had been making. At first, they were just that, rumours, but then the video of Lucy Shaffer surfaced on websites. If that video existed, the odds were pretty good the rumours were true. Stella entered her office with this on her mind.

"How can I help you?" she said as she walked into her office.

"I'm here on personal business," Calvin said as he got up from the chair in front of Stella's desk.

Calvin's face flushed with embarrassment, but he extended a hand and tried to muster his best smile. With his black eye the smile came off as a bit creepy, but Stella was used to seeing such forced smiles. She knew right away which addiction the young man before her was here about. Once seated she noticed eye contact was difficult for him, as he looked at his hands more often than not.

"The normal procedure would be to book a counselling session with one of the therapists," Stella stated, watching Calvin's body language. "I'm no therapist. I manage the day to day side of things and not the actual therapy."

"I know, but—" Calvin paused, wiping his sweaty palms on his pants as he spoke. "I just want to make sure that my coming here would be confidential. I can't have this getting out."

"I see," Stella said as she leaned forward against the desk, steepling her fingers before her.

"I could lose my job if this got out," Calvin said. He made brief eye contact and then looked at his hands again.

"We try our best to keep things as confidential as possible here at the centre. But with that said, you have to remember that Poplar Falls is not that big a town."

"I know," Calvin replied. He lowered his gaze to the breasts resting on the desk before him.

Stella noticed his gaze and leaned forward more to increase the way her breasts were being pushed upwards, emphasising her cleavage. She watched as Calvin squirmed in his chair.

"You're Calvin Crawford, aren't you?" Stella asked.

"I'm a porn addict," Calvin blurted. "Please don't tell anyone."

"We're very discreet here at the clinic," Stella said.

"Thank God," Calvin said, and he stole another glance at the cleavage resting across the desk from him.

"Speaking of discretion—just between you and me, are the rumours true?"

"What rumours?"

"Was Charlie filming himself having sex with women?"

Calvin's lack of answer was more answer than any lie he might have tried to come up with. Calvin shifted uneasily in his chair and stole another glance at the busty woman who sat across from him. He felt small, like he was in school again, sexually crushing on his homeroom teacher.

"Calvin? Have you seen me naked?"

Calvin blushed fiercely. Stella smiled at him. Her smile was mischievous and Calvin suddenly felt his stomach churn. He really had come to the clinic for help and this was not what he had in mind.

"Are you married? Girlfriend?"

"No," Calvin replied.

"Is it true that there are videos of Charlie having sex?" Stella asked. "Am I in any of those videos? I'd hate for my momma to see those but she's all confused now, living in Sleepy Meadows over in Carlton."

"You know I can't discuss an open investigation, right?"

"Look, Calvin. I can make you an appointment with one of our therapists under a fake name, if that's what you want. I do it all the time, usually for rich folks who want to keep it secret."

Calvin shifted in his chair and resumed eye contact but didn't speak as he listened on.

"That or we can help each other out," Stella added. "It's no secret that I've been crazy lonely since Charlie died. And as you probably know by now, I fell off the wagon, hard. So I got a proposition for you."

"What are you saying?" Calvin asked as he swallowed nervously.

"I'm thinking you and I should hook up," Stella said as her eyes roamed over the young man before her. "That way, you can help me forget Charlie and I can help you forget about porn for a while. I mean, we're both grown ups and I'm really trying hard not to reach for a bottle, but it's difficult, Calvin. It's very difficult, especially when I get lonely."

Calvin blushed and looked at Stella's breasts, and made eye contact to see Stella smiling at him.

"Are you... are you a virgin?" Stella asked. Her smile was replaced with an inquisitive look.

"No," Calvin replied. "No, I'm not."

The truth was Calvin had been a virgin until college, where he met a confused young woman whom he dated for a few months. His ideas about what sex was stemmed from porn, so their sex life was awkward and short-lived. Now Calvin found himself sitting across from a busty black woman who wanted to have sex with him and he didn't know what to do about it. He knew she was probably right about one thing: If they had sex then it might help him with his porn addiction.

"I can see you're not too sure what to say to my proposal," Stella said as she got up from behind the desk and walked to the office door.

Calvin stood and followed, assuming Stella was ending their meeting. But Stella instead lowered the blind in the window of the door and locked it before turning to face Calvin. She undid a button on her blouse, exposing herself more as Calvin watched intensely.

She smiled as she spoke. "Let me give you something to think about," she said, continuing to unbutton her blouse.

49

Marci Grant stood in her tight-fitting business suit and heels on the porch of a small bungalow on Peach Street, digging through her purse for her phone. Tucked under her arm was a beige folder containing the signed documents for the house she had just listed under Red Realty. Marci needed to call her friend Dave, who was a woodworker and did all of her sign work as well. Soon, Dave would be installing a new sign on the front lawn of this very bungalow on Peach Street. As Marci dug through her large red purse, a thought crossed her mind to ask Dave about this new guy he'd been seeing.

Just as Marci's gloved fingers felt the familiar feel of her phone, it began the familiar song from the sitcom which she knew so well.

Soft Kitty, Warm Kitty...

"Hey, sexy," Marci answered cheerfully. She was always happy after landing new customers, and a happy Marci meant a playful Marci.

"Hey," Trudy replied. "Is this a bad time?"

"Not at all, I just signed a house," Marci replied gleefully.

"That's good," Trudy replied.

Marci paused for a moment, expecting Trudy to say something, but got silence instead. "What's on your mind?" Trudy sounded odd and this usually meant a fight brewing;

although she sounded depressed and not confrontational.

"I was thinking we should go away somewhere," Trudy replied. "I know we talked about a cruise, but I was thinking maybe a trip."

"Where?"

"Mexico. Just you and me. Just get away from it all," Trudy replied.

"But what about your daughter?"

"She'll stay at her dad's while we're away. I already asked him," Trudy replied, apparently having thought it through.

"I'd love to go away with you," Marci replied. "But right now? I just signed a house and we're in peak season for showing houses. I have six showings this week alone, not to mention the Blanchards left me a voicemail about the Turlington house."

"You'd say yes if you really loved me," Trudy blurted.

"I do love you and you know that," Marci replied firmly. "But you know how slow winter is in my business and so I've got to take all the work I can get when it's there. I promise we'll go to Mexico this winter, just you and me."

"You wouldn't say no to the porn-making slut, Lucy Shaffer," Trudy replied. Her voice sounded as if she was ready to cry, just before ending the call.

"Hello? Hello?" Marci pulled her phone away from her ear and looked at it to see if the call had really ended.

Soon after, Marci sat in her red Corvette and opened a web browser on her phone and tapped three words.

Lucy Shaffer porn.

A tabloid site popped up first, confirming what she had suspected. Charlie Baker had filmed himself with Lucy Shaffer after all. And now it was on the internet. Marci smirked at the idea of the Shaffer video being on porn sites. She wondered if the rumours she heard about the laptop they found were true. She had heard it was busted but that they had managed to fix it. Most likely the rumours were true. And if someone knew if they were true, it would be Dave. Dave gave new meaning to the term 'getting wood'.

50

Many of the kids at Sunshine and Rainbows Daycare couldn't leave without a hug from Sadie Cross. Lately most parents looked at Sadie differently, ever since the rumours of her affair with the promiscuous Charlie Baker spread throughout town. But the demure little woman hadn't changed in the eyes of the kids she took such good care of. During her days at work, those kids were everything. Sure, sometimes Sadie might get frustrated but she never took it out on the kids. She loved them all, equally. Well, almost equally. Every once in a while, there would be one to test her, and recently it had been Anna, the little girl who always wore pigtails and fought with all the boys. But even though Anna was difficult, Sadie still had a place for her in her heart. It was almost as good as having children of her own, something she and her husband had never been able to do. Lord knows they had tried.

In the early years of their marriage, Sadie had insisted on having at least two kids. But unable to conceive, she dedicated her life to taking care of other people's kids by starting her very own daycare. Even when she felt her marriage failing, growing apart from her husband, the kids would always fill her heart with joy. But as time passed loneliness set in, and then came Charlie Baker. The first time she met Charlie was at a Jabba-da-Java Coffee Hut. She was getting coffee for herself and her staff. Charlie had always looked for ways to strike up a conversation with any women who caught his eye, and Sadie did just that. So the partially-eaten large slab of dark chocolate sticking out of this little demure woman's purse was the perfect conversation starter. Soon she was blushing and giggling at his jokes, perhaps more than she should have. But this handsome man had some pretty good guesses as to why she would need such a large amount of dark chocolate on hand at all times. And when he suggested she try the Magnolia Wellness and Rehabilitation Centre, she naturally assumed he worked there. He suggested they could help her kick her addiction to chocolate and perhaps help with why she felt she needed to have said chocolate. Sadie, being a proper married woman, brushed off the flirtatious man she had just met, but couldn't forget him. He had flirted with her, not in a sexual way but with his eyes and his smile. He had made her feel attractive without being too forward. Soon after, Sadie found herself trying to bump into the man she had met at the coffee shop.

But now she noticed the way the parents acted around her when picking up their children. The kids themselves hadn't changed at all. Little Thomas ran to Sadie, opened his arms, and smiled as he looked up at her. Lemkie watched from the door as his son got a big hug from the demure little woman. The same woman he had always envisioned as the ideal daycare owner. She had always reminded him of that Poppins woman from that Disney flick. But after seeing video footage of her with Charlie Baker, he just couldn't meld what he had seen with the women he now watched hugging his son. Sadie crouched down and Thomas hugged her hard, his little feet lifted off the floor in the process. He smiled wide as the daycare owner set him down and watched him run to his father at the door. He wrapped his little arms around his father's leg and smiled.

Lemkie watched as a little girl in pigtails tugged on Sadie's sweater, and waited open-armed for her turn to hug the beloved daycare owner. Sadie smiled as she hugged the little girl, tickling her as she did so. The little girl squealed in delight as she pushed Sadie away, escaping the tickling that she was enjoying more than she let on. Sadie straightened herself to find the little girl's father standing before her, wanting a hug of his own. Something that Sadie brushed off as nonsense, as hugs were reserved only for the kids. But the father stepped in and hugged her anyway. And from where Lemkie stood, he could see the man mouth something to the daycare owner as he stole his unwanted hug. Sadie stepped back, eyes wide, and slapped the man across the face. Lemkie watched as the shocked and embarrassed man picked up his daughter and quickly exited the daycare.

Lemkie marvelled as he watched Sadie quickly regain her composure and turn her attention to the kids as if nothing had happened. She was amazing with those kids, thought Lemkie as he left, carrying his son who was now regaling him with stories of his adventures in daycare. But Lemkie wasn't listening to his son; instead he was trying hard to associate the demure woman who was so good with kids with the passionate woman he had seen in the Charlie Baker video footage.

51

Her gloves off, Marci Grant sat at her desk in her Red Realty downtown office. A space she rented in the only commercial property owned by Agatha Tilley. A building she'd love to own and Agatha has agreed to sell her for the right price. And by the end of the summer, Marci figured on having the down payment she needed to make the deal. But now alone in her rented office, late that afternoon, she was about to find what she had been looking for and she wanted privacy when she did. Trudy always hovered a lot when she was on her home computer, and so the office with her laptop was the best place for privacy. Especially when you were searching the internet for porn. But this time, before she could search further, the very first search result would pique her interest. The headline of the article on the tabloid website told a new story.

'Lucy Shaffer fires agent Doris Davis'. The article briefly mentioned it being over allegations of her being involved in the leaked sex tape.

After regretting clicking on the article and fighting off a slew of pop-ups, Marci gave up on reading that article and got back to her original mission which was finding the video of Lucy Shaffer naked; better yet, having sex. Today she would finally admit it even if it was only to herself, that Trudy did have valid reason to be jealous about her fascination with the Hollywood star. She clicked on the site which was supposedly to have the video she so desperately wanted to watch, only to have a pop-up block her view, and clicking on it to get rid of it caused her screen to freeze at first. A moment later, a black screen covered in text popped up and disappeared just as fast. Her computer crashed before it could upload the virus. She assumed that was what had just happened as blinding rage filled her. Furious, she grappled with the laptop and flung it into the nearest wall, smashing it open in the process and watching as it crashed to the floor.

Marci gripped the arms of her chair, breathing deeply in an attempt to calm herself. She looked at the hole in the drywall where the computer had made contact. The laptop lay face down on the floor with a part of it cracked open, the I key on the floor next to it. Good thing Charlie Baker, who helped her install a security camera in her office, had recommended she keep her files on an external hard drive like he did. It was a lot harder to lose your data that way.

"Fuck!" Marci exclaimed as she wondered if she could get a new laptop of the same brand so Trudy wouldn't notice. Once she had calmed down a little, she would wonder how to fix the hole in the wall before anyone could find out about it. Maybe Dave could help, she thought. But first she needed a new laptop, and fast.

52

Sadie pulled the door open hard as she barged into Vernon's Meats, trying to vent some of her anger. She stood with her back to the door, waiting to hear it slam, when all she heard was the hissing of the cylinder at the top of the door, doing its job as the door eased closed. Sadie turned and stopped the door before it could fully close, opened it, and yanked on it again only to have the cylinder foil her plan yet again. Frustrated, she grasped the door's handle and pulled hard. She grunted, gave it her all, as her feet slipped up from under her and she lost her grasp on the handle, falling flat on her ass. She kicked at the door but the soft-soled shoe she wore when at work had no effect on the closed door. She scrambled to her feet, dusted herself off and turned to see the young cashier who worked part time, gawking at her as she held out a plastic bag in front of her.

Geraldine, the wife of Pastor George, stood across the counter frozen in place. She was obviously stunned at what they had just witnessed. She clutched her purse tightly and gave Sadie a wide berth as she made her way out of the shop.

"That'll give those old bitches something to talk about while they fucking knit," Sadie blurted, her face flushed.

The young girl with the pierced lower lip set down the bag Geraldine had forgotten to take with her as she spoke. "Geraldine forgot her bag. Um, I'm going to take my break now if that's okay." The girl, whose name Sadie couldn't remember, didn't wait for Vernon to answer as she scooped up her iPhone from beneath the counter and left as quickly as she could.

That's when Sadie saw Vernon peeking from the opening that looked in to the kitchen. He was wiping his eyes with the sleeve of his shirt as he spoke.

"What the hell got into you?" he said coldly.

Sadie knew he would have something to say about her

entrance and about the bits of chocolate in her teeth. She could feel it on her front teeth but simply didn't care. She was angry and the more she stewed over it all, the angrier she got. She watched Vernon disappear into the kitchen again and she could hear the knife on the cutting board.

The variety of scents overwhelmed her as she barged into the kitchen; she puffed as she threw her purse on the counter and watched as Vernon went back to cutting up onions, tears streaming down his face. He blinked a few times and then held his eyes shut for a moment as he waited for his eyesight to clear up. On the island were mounds of chopped up green and red peppers. He was working on the onions as he made what looked like his best seller, his meatloaf. That explained the scents, Sadie briefly thought.

"You should have heard what that fucker said to me," Sadie stated. "And with his daughter standing right next to me, on top of that."

"Who are we talking about?" Vernon asked as he squinted at the onions he was cutting again.

"That Nathan Bourque guy I told you about; the father of that rough little girl who always picks on Thomas."

"What about him?" Vernon asked as he peeled more onions for chopping.

"He said he had a big dick, too, and would love to fuck me with it," Sadie blurted. "Can you believe that? What the fuck does he think I am, a slut?" Sadie pointed at Vernon. "Don't answer that!"

"Well, people are talking, Sadie. It's not like you did a good job of hiding the fact that you were screwing Charlie Baker."

"Are you fucking serious?" Sadie replied, raising her voice in anger. "You're going to lecture me about not hiding my infidelities properly? You know, everyone in town knows you're gay."

Vernon tried to look at his wife but his vision was still

blurred by tears from the onions. A fact he didn't mind since he wasn't sure how he could avoid becoming emotional about finally having this conversation with his best friend.

"I..." Vernon began before being cut off.

"Don't you fucking dare deny it," Sadie said as she dug through her purse to find the small piece of dark chocolate she had in there somewhere.

"This is not how I wanted to have this conversation," Vernon replied as he peeled the last of the onions and discarded the peel into a bowl for the compost pile at home.

Sadie dug out the small piece of dark chocolate from her purse, removed the foil from it, and shoved the entire piece into her mouth. She balled up the foil wrapper and tossed it into Vernon's compost bowl.

"I never wanted to hurt you," Vernon said as he choked back his emotions. "Besides, I can't come out."

"Why the fuck not?" Sadie asked as she tried to savour her chocolate.

"It'll hurt my business."

"Are you fucking kidding me?"

"It's true," Vernon replied. "Say what you want, but people wouldn't buy anything from me if they knew I was gay."

"That's what you're worried about?" Sadie replied. "Not me, but your fucking store? I'm your *wife*, for God's sake. But you're worried people won't buy your fancy sausages anymore."

"That's not what I meant and you know it," Vernon blurted, clearly upset. He took a stainless steel bowl and scooped green peppers into it and transferred that into an even larger stainless steel bowl. "But I've worked hard to build this business."

"You're an asshole," Sadie blurted as she turned and marched off down a small hallway towards the back office. Wanting to calm herself somewhat, she paced back and forth in the dimly lit office in the back of Vernon's Meats.

At least he had finally admitted it to her. He had finally said it. After all the years of wondering, she had decided it must have been true many years ago. But finally discussing it should have been a relief and yet somehow it wasn't. She supposed that had they had this discussion prior to Charlie Baker entering her life, she could have used the infidelity against him. But Charlie and his big dick and charming personality had taken that from her. She was just as guilty of cheating as he was. Maybe not for as long, but just as guilty and they both knew it.

Divorce was the only answer. She would keep her business and he would keep his. That seemed fair, she thought. She thought his was worth more since he had less overhead, but she couldn't worry about that. She wouldn't allow herself to worry about that. She could finally date again. Date men who were attracted to her sexually. But that did mean leaving Vernon and he really was her best friend. A tear flowed down her cheek as she stopped pacing. That's when she noticed the new wooden lamp on Vernon's office desk.

The lamp had a large beige lampshade which helped it cast its soft glow across the otherwise sombre office. She would remember this lamp had she seen it before. In the next few days, when asked why she had done what she did next, she honestly wouldn't know why she did it. But she flicked the switch to turn off the lamp only it didn't go off. Instead it cast an even dimmer light but on the wall next to the lamp it cast a shadow. A clearly distinct shadow she recognized as being very male. She froze as she looked at the shadow in disbelief. And sticking out from under the lamp's ornate varnished wood base was a note.

I made this especially for you.
Dave
XOX

Sadie picked up the lamp, yanked at the cord, plucking it out of the wall, and walked back to the kitchen.

"Who the fuck is Dave?"

Vernon, who had combined the peppers and onions into a large steel bowl, was in the process of cracking eggs while tears still flowed due to the strong onions in the bowl.

"Put that back," Vernon blurted, slamming down the knife he chopped onions with.

Sadie was holding his new lamp as she stood in the doorway of his kitchen.

"I'm not concealing my fling with Charlie well enough, you said. What the fuck is this dick lamp doing in your office?"

"It's a gift. Now go put that back where you found it," Vernon replied as he accidentally knocked eggs off the island. Four eggs fell at first, followed by another which slowly rolled off the island and cracked on the floor with the rest.

"Did he shove it up your fucking ass?" Sadie asked as she waved the lamp around, almost knocking the shade off in the process.

"Put that back before you break it, you bitch," Vernon replied. "That's hand- made."

"Hand-made? Gives new meaning to having wood doesn't it, you fucking asshole!"

Vernon normally would have thought those jokes were pretty funny. But right this minute, he was more concerned about his angry wife damaging his new lamp that he loved dearly.

"You're going to damage it," Vernon said. "Put that back where you got it, now!" he demanded.

"Fuck you," Sadie replied as she slammed it down over her right knee. The lamp made a loud snapping sound and broke in two very pointy halves, splitting along the wood grain. She felt a sharp pain in her knee followed by a light-headedness, as the lamp had been much harder than she imagined.

"You FUCKING BITCH," Vernon shouted, and took a step towards his wife and slipped in the mess of broken eggs on the floor. He flailed his arms to balance himself and lurched forward. He grasped at her shoulders to keep from falling. As their bodies crashed together, Vernon felt a sharp pain in his side as he and his wife both staggered. The process slammed the end of the broken lamp against the wall, driving the other end into Vernon's abdomen. He stopped and looked at the base of the lamp protruding from his stomach. The lamp shade slipped off the upper end Sadie still clutched in her other hand. The shade fell to the floor and rolled into the broken eggs.

"Fuck!" Vernon said. "You fucking stabbed me."

"It was an accident," Sadie stated as she looked at the base of the lamp protruding from her husband's stomach. She looked at the top half of the lamp in her hand, two of the four bulbs broken in the sockets. With the shade off, she could see the very top was an intricately carved, vein-covered, wooden dick.

"Fuck that," Vernon replied. "Everybody in town is going to say you tried to kill me."

"What?"

"After the way you came in here today," Vernon replied, and his hands began to shake as he gently wrapped them around the bottom half of the lamp which was beginning to get slick with blood. His face still wet with tears from the onions. "And it won't matter what I say either. People will say I tried to cover for you if I say you didn't."

"Are you serious?" Sadie replied, visibly shaken as she looked at her empty hand, covered in her husband's blood.

"Call 911," Vernon said. "I need an ambulance."

"You seriously think people will think I tried to kill you?" Sadie asked. "That's what worries you, isn't it?"

"I'm bleeding, Sadie. You stabbed me with my fucking

lamp."

"It was an accident, you fuck-nut."

"Just fucking call 911, you chocolate-eating bitch!"

"FUCK YOU," Sadie shouted as she stabbed Vernon in the gut with the other half of the lamp. She scraped her own arm with a piece of broken glass from the bulb as she did, but never felt it cut her.

Vernon staggered back and slipped in a combination of blood and eggs, and fell flat on his back, hitting his head in the process. He groaned and touched the back of his head, checking his hand and seeing blood.

"I should have left you years ago, you crazy bitch," Vernon murmured as he squirmed on the floor, writhing in pain from the stab wounds and the blow to the head.

Sadie screamed in anger as she wrapped her hands around the top half of the lamp, grasping the wooden dick like a wooden stake, and plunged it into her husband's chest as hard as she could, breaking the two remaining bulbs in the process. Furious with years of pent-up anger, she screamed at him while she half straddled him, bearing down on the bloody wooden dick protruding out of his chest. That's when she heard the shrill scream coming from the kitchen door leading to the front of the meat market. Standing there was the young cashier with the pierced lip, shrieking loudly. Behind her, pale-faced and peering over her shoulder was Geraldine, the wife of Pastor George.

Sadie looked at her shaking, blood-covered hands in disbelief as the largest chocolate craving of her life washed over her. As she tried to stand, her knees buckled and her head spun. Sadie blacked out before she hit the floor.

53

Geraldine trembled as she sat in her car, her old Nokia

flip phone in her hand as she scrolled through her contacts. Finding Emma, she dialled and the phone rang twice.

"Hello?" she heard Emma say.

Emma, dressed in a nun's habit, was in her kitchen, getting a drink of water. The role-playing was getting to be thirsty work. Emma set down her riding crop, swapping it for her glass, and took another sip of water with the cordless phone at her ear.

"You're not going to believe me when I tell you," Geraldine blurted.

"Geraldine? Is that you?"

"Sadie just killed Vernon. At least I think he's dead. He has to be. God. No way he could survive that." Geraldine was rambling nervously.

"What?" Emma inquired, not sure her hearing wasn't failing her at this moment. "Say that again." Emma sat at her kitchen table with her glass of water and her cordless phone.

"Stabbed him to death with a dildo, I think."

"A what?"

"I know what I saw," Geraldine said. "It looked like a dick, I'm telling you. It had to be a dildo." She shook nervously, adrenaline pumping as she spoke.

"Tell me everything," Emma replied excitedly.

"You coming back or what?" she heard Bill shout from the basement.

Bill could wait, thought Emma. It's not like he was in any position to do anything but wait anyway. She had bound him good this time. Mind you, the bindings weren't tight enough to cut off circulation or anything, but he'd be held in place for a bit. Plus the Viagra had only kicked in a half hour ago, so that would last a few more hours. He could wait, she thought as she listened to Geraldine tell her what had happened that afternoon at Vernon's Meats.

54

The paramedics had arrived in time to find Sadie as she regained consciousness and were forced to sedate her when she became frantic at the sight of her dead husband. Officers struggled to hold her down as the paramedics injected a sedative. They were in the process of wheeling her out, strapped to a stretcher, when Detective Tilley arrived.

"Where's Dodge?" Lemkie asked moments later. He winced from the strong smell of onions which overpowered the other smells of bodily fluids, peppers, and other various foods. The pair stood at the kitchen door of Vernon's Meats, marvelling at the sight before them. Vernon lay dead in a large pool of blood and broken eggs, the murder weapon still protruding from his chest.

"I don't know," Detective Tilley replied as she waved away some of the smell. "He asked if I needed him right away and I said no. I told him this was pretty cut and dry. Vernon's dead and witnesses saw Sadie kill him."

"Yeah," Lemkie replied. "No mystery to solve here, that's for sure. Although I wonder what made her snap and kill him. I mean, she looked a little agitated at the daycare, but I didn't think she looked upset enough to kill anyone."

"Did you see the murder weapon?" Tilley asked as she nudged Lemkie with her elbow.

"Yeah," Lemkie replied pointing at a lampshade on the floor. "My bet is that's part of that. Hard to tell with all the blood but it looks like a wooden dildo; if it wasn't for the light sockets sticking out, that is."

"You men and your infatuation with your dicks," Tilley replied.

Lemkie smiled at first, then chuckled, and Tilley shook her head in disbelief.

"Who says it wasn't hers?" Lemkie said.

"Dodge said he'd get here as soon as possible," Tilley

said, ignoring Lemkie's comment. "And the chief's gonna love this one, too."

"Yeah, well, they're not gonna believe this one," Lemkie replied. "Especially not after the way we found Charlie Baker."

"Yeah, he's been complaining about how long we've been taking. How long Calvin's been taking on those videos, too. He won't enjoy the idea of us getting sidetracked again."

55

Dodge ended the call from Detective Tilley as he stood in the parking lot of the recycling centre. He tucked his Blackberry into his pocket as he pondered the news of Sadie killing her husband. And from what Tilley said, she did this in his own store of all places. Stabbed him, and he couldn't help but wonder what had brought that on. What would make the demure little daycare owner snap and stab someone? She had seemed a bit unstable when they first met to ask questions about Charlie Baker, but murdering her own husband? Maybe she did kill Charlie Baker after all, thought Dodge. Shaking his head out of the fog he found himself in, he tried to refocus on the task at hand. After all, he was perhaps going to finally get answers he'd needed for a long time now. Dodge wasn't the type to lose sleep over anything, but he would definitely feel better once he knew.

He watched Walter unload his trailer and bring Thursday's haul inside the recycling depot. Dodge reached into his back pocket and pulled out an empty pint of whiskey; empty save for the rolled up paper on the inside of the bottle. Using a tissue, he wiped down the clear glass bottle as he went inside.

He watched Walter stand before the counting station of the recycling depot as the clerk counted each can, bottle, and cardboard container. Walter watched intensely as the clerk counted quickly, hurrying along.

Dodge couldn't help but notice Walter looked thinner than ever. He looked sickly. Walter pulled at his pants to keep them from sliding down to his buttocks. Dodge smiled, a little amused at the thought that some kids wore their pants like this thinking they looked cool. Walter looked emaciated, and so now even with a belt his dirty pants were falling off him. His smile vanished as he made a mental note about Walter's health.

The clerk finished his count and scribbled on a notepad, tallying up the recyclables as Walter watched. Dodge walked up behind Walter and held out the whiskey bottle to the brain-damaged young man.

"Walter," Dodge said, getting his attention. "You dropped one." He held out the bottle for Walter to take, which he did.

"Wednesday," Walter said with a puzzled look as he took the bottle from Dodge. Walter turned, handed the bottle with the rolled-up paper inside it to the clerk, who examined it and looked at Dodge before lightly tossing it into the glass bottle bin. The clerk scratched out the count on the paper and tallied it again. The clerk walked Walter over to the cash register and handed the paper to Mr. O'Neil, who up until then had been paying no attention to any of them. He took the paper from the clerk and proceeded to pay Walter the money owed him.

Dodge, satisfied that Walter was no longer paying him any heed, reached into the glass bottle bin and fished out the whiskey bottle with the note inside it. He grasped it by the neck of the bottle and shot a satisfied glance at the clerk. The clerk wore thick rubber gloves but Walter's hands were bare as usual. Dodge pulled a plastic bag from his pocket, slipped the bottle inside it, and left.

56

The morning after Sadie killed her husband, Calvin sat alone in the lab going through the Charlie Baker files on his laptop, earbuds in place while he listened to the calming saxophone music of Kenny G on his phone. Calvin hadn't been this relaxed since before he moved to Poplar Falls and took the job as a crime scene investigator.

Being a CSI looked exciting and glamorous on television, but he'd learned it wasn't so when he started on the path studying Forensic Science. Many times he doubted whether this was the career for him, but he was good at it; in fact, he was more than good. Maybe he wasn't the best in class, but considering that he never studied at all and still did very well he decided to stay the course, literally and figuratively. But studying and actually working turned out to be completely different things. When you worked a real case, you were directly affecting people's lives.

The Panty Bandit case wasn't that big a deal because he didn't take the case seriously. This was something he never told anyone because they wouldn't understand. To Calvin it wasn't that the women's safety wasn't a concern, but that all the Bandit did was steal dirty underwear. To Calvin, that was petty. But now he was working on a murder investigation and the pressure was immense. Not to mention that as a porn addict, the last thing he wanted was to have to watch porn for the job. But Stella had been right when she said she could help him. Mind you, the type of help she gave Calvin wasn't normally how they helped clients at the wellness centre. This sort of help would get her fired if someone found out. But it turned out to be exactly what Calvin needed. And turns out that Stella knew a whole lot about work-related stress. After a session of rigorous sex, and a few hours of conversation, Calvin realised that he was the only one putting all the pressure on him. Now Calvin sat, watching short clips of Charlie Baker's home movies, skipping through parts and selectively watching others while sipping a can of Red Bull.

As Calvin clicked on a file, convinced he had already seen it before, he clicked the time strip to start the video about midway through its run. Stella had suggested that he should try other ways to ease the tension he had been creating for himself. She had mentioned that music could help take his mind off of things. And Stella had been right, this music was calming. So as Kenny G's soothing melodies played on, Calvin leaned back and sipped his Red Bull.

It was while sipping Red Bull that Calvin realized what he was watching as he gasped, choked on the caffeinated drink, and sprayed the sticky liquid all over the monitor. Calvin coughed, spat and, using the handy box of tissues, blew his nose while he struggled to regain his breath.

Calvin realized that in this video, Charlie was tied to the bed like they had found him. He restarted the video and began watching again, this time much more intently. The angle of the video meant it had to be from the bizarre statue of a rabbit that Charlie had perched atop the television on a stand. On the screen, other than his mouthful of Red Bull and spittle was a blonde woman, her back to the camera. She was down to her matching bra and panties, standing at the foot of the bed. In her hand she held a thick rope that Calvin instantly recognized from the mountains of evidence they had catalogued. At this point in the video, Charlie lay on the bed with his hands already bound to the metal four- post bedframe. The blonde woman was in the process of tying his right foot. Charlie mouthed something, which is when Calvin realised Kenny G was still playing in his ears. He ripped out the earbuds and quickly set his phone aside. He then remembered that the videos from this angle had no sound and, combined with the angle of Charlie's head, made it impossible to discern what he was saying.

The one thing that was obvious was that Charlie being

tied up had been consensual. The fact that he wasn't struggling was the first hint, the second was the large erection, and a third was the smile on Charlie's face. All this clearly meant this was not being done against his will. Charlie glanced around the room as his right hand flexed a little. Calvin could only guess that Charlie hadn't had the chance to activate all his cameras for this one and was now wishing he had. Calvin recalled a small broken remote that looked as if someone had stepped on it. Charlie lay completely naked and fully erect as the woman finished tying his foot. She slowly walked around the side of the bed but somehow she remained turned away from the camera, and this frustrated Calvin who was now leaning forward as if it would help him see better.

Charlie Baker's smile had faded but his erection remained. Calvin knew this was because of the bottle of pills precariously perched on the edge of the nightstand. Even with the powerful camera being zoomed in on the bed, there was no way of knowing what the pills would have been had he not been there to see for himself.

The blonde woman, still in her matching lace underwear, climbed onto the bed and straddled Charlie, sitting on his stomach while ignoring his large, erect manhood. Calvin could only assume they were talking as she sat on Charlie Baker for a good thirty seconds, maybe more. The camera angle showed Charlie's hands clenching and tensing against the ropes. Calvin could only assume the conversation might not have been as pleasant and charming as Charlie Baker was accustomed to. Stella had told him about how truly charming the man had been. But Calvin had a feeling that Charlie Baker's charm had no effect on this woman. The blonde reached for a pillow and Calvin leaned even closer to the screen, only to watch it go blank.

Calvin sat back in disbelief as the hiss of the speakers was still there and the lights on the laptop still lit. He checked and the laptop was still plugged as it had been. But with the blacked-out screen, he could now see just how much Red Bull he had spewed when he first saw the blonde with the rope.

"Fuck me," he said aloud.

It took a few minutes to find one, but Calvin fetched another monitor from one of the lab's desktop computers and connected it to the laptop. Shortly after doing so he was viewing the video from the laptop via the monitor. Calvin's stomach churned and the urge to vomit returned as he saw the video footage was still playing, but now Charlie lay still, covered by a thin silk blanket with a crumpled pillow on his face. He moved the media player back to about where he thought he was when it had blanked out. Again, he saw the woman walk around to the side of the bed and straddle Charlie's stomach. Again he watched them, assuming they were talking. Again, the blonde woman reached for the pillow, but this time the screen didn't go blank and she grabbed it.

Charlie's hands clenched and unclenched multiple times, and his feet twitched as much as the rope would allow. The woman seemed to fidget some with the pillow held at chest height. She leaned forward, pressing the pillow on Charlie's face, leaning into it with all her weight applied to the pillow. Charlie bucked against the ropes, to no avail. Something Calvin already knew since he knew the ending of Charlie Baker's story. He watched Charlie struggle hard at first, weaken, and eventually stop struggling altogether. The blonde woman sat up, leaving the pillow on her victim's face. She seemed to hesitate there for a moment as if already regretting her actions, Calvin assumed. She swung her leg backwards as she climbed off Charlie, knocking his manhood around in the process. Calvin watched it bob and weave for a moment before he realized that in doing so she had finally turned towards the rabbit eye camera, which recorded everything but sound. He watched as the woman he recognized as Trudy

Wilkins picked up a thin off-white blanket and draped it over Charlie Baker's torso. Why she did this, Calvin wanted to ask her. It didn't really make sense to him, but he thought he saw regret written all over her face. He remembered reading the term "crime of passion" a lot in class. Although this wasn't what he had pictured when he read that terminology it certainly fit the bill, he thought.

He watched her as she dressed, moving outside of the camera's view as she did. A few shadows were enough to show she was near the bed for a few brief moments. Shortly after there was a flash of daylight, which Calvin assumed was the front door opening and closing as Trudy Wilkins left the scene of the crime.

Still half-watching Charlie Baker with the pillow on his face as the camera had kept recording, Calvin grabbed the phone and called Lemkie who answered his cell phone on the third ring.

"You'll never believe what I just found," Calvin blurted.

57

Dodge and Tilley sat in chairs flanking Lemkie, who sat in front of the external monitor and laptop combination which he didn't bother explaining to the detectives. The fact that Calvin had sprayed Red Bull all over it seemed irrelevant at this point, especially since they had just finished watching the murder of Charlie Baker. The video played on but nothing moved on the screen. Charlie lay with the crumpled pillow still on his face, his fully erect manhood under the silk blanket.

"Where's Calvin?" Detective Tilley inquired, leaning back with her arms folded against her stomach.

"After he showed me the video he threw up all over himself, so I sent him home," Lemkie replied.

"Sheesh," Dodge replied. "He looked fine when he came in this morning; more than fine actually. I've never seen him look so chipper."

"Me either, although he has been acting strange this last week," Lemkie added as he stopped the media player. "I'll put a copy of this in the Q drive for you," he added while looking at Tilley.

"Thanks," she replied.

"I can't believe it was that easy," Dodge said. "Although it did take him a long damn time to hack into that video."

"Actually, about that," Lemkie replied. "I've been meaning to talk to the both of you about that. To be honest, Calvin had hacked everything a long time ago. Probably a day or two after we collected the drives. The same goes for the laptop. But he left out the part about the metadata being corrupt."

"The what?" Dodge asked. "English please?"

"It's like file-cataloguing information," Tilley said. "Including when it was recorded."

"Exactly," Lemkie replied as he pushed his chair away from the desk so he could better see the detectives as he spoke. "Anyway, we never assumed Charlie would have recorded his own death. I mean, Calvin was compiling a list of suspects, which is all we assumed we'd get from all the footage. And the only reason it took so long to go through it all is he kept having to stop to help me collect and catalogue evidence. I think he thought we wouldn't notice, but I know computers way better than he assumes I do."

"I'm not following you," Dodge said.

"Calvin had the files hacked long ago. He lied about not having them all hacked. But I saw no harm in that since I needed him to view the content and I knew that's what he was doing anyway. To be honest, I'm not sure why he lied about that part but I sort of went along with it."

"What do you mean, sorta went along with it?" Tilley asked.

"Well, in the beginning I needed him on the tech stuff since I had so much potential evidence to go over. Plus, there was so much of it. The homemade porn. And I could tell he was getting pretty stressed out about it all, but I thought that was just because we teased him about watching Charlie Baker's porn," Lemkie said. "Either way, I knew he was going through the files, compiling pictures and lists. He had done a good chunk of the files on the portable hard drives, but you have to understand that Charlie had four cameras in his place. That means potentially four videos for each of his rendezvous," Lemkie added.

"So you were monitoring him?" Dodge asked.

"Of course," Lemkie replied in a sarcastic tone. "I am his boss, after all. But the Panty Bandit fingerprints on the laptop threw me right off, I have to admit."

"Which reminds me," Dodge said, glancing at Tilley as he continued speaking to Lemkie. "I have to tell you about that."

Lemkie looked puzzled at that statement but went on. "Anyway, I have to admit I started worrying about Calvin's work on this case when I found vomit in the lab. And I was going to say something to you guys but wanted to keep this hush-hush until I knew for sure."

"For sure?" Tilley asked.

"For sure that it was him who leaked the Lucy Shaffer video," Lemkie replied.

"What?" Dodge replied.

"I think Lucy's agent paid him to do it," Lemkie added. "But I need proof. Besides, I'm worried that if that got out then the rest of the case would be considered contaminated, so I kept that to myself for now."

"Good idea," Dodge replied.

"Also, I noticed something odd today which I was going to ask him about, but he sprang this on me before I could," Lemkie said. "I noticed he deleted Stella Rubbin from the list of suspects. He deleted the videos of her, too."

"You know this how?" Tilley asked.

"How do you want me to forget that list of women?" he said with a smirk. "Besides, I made back up copies of all the files long ago just to be sure. The Stella videos are gone from his folders, but I still have copies."

Dodge looked at him with his usual raised eyebrow look that exuded confusion.

"I was looking through the files, trying to come up with a way to ask him about the hacked files. I'm pretty sure he used a USB, but being the computer wiz he is he covered his tracks well. I know the hack story is bullshit. Just like the story about taking this long to hack all the videos."

"Good to know," Tilley replied. "Well, we should probably go track down Trudy Wilkins since we now know she's the one who murdered Charlie Baker."

"True," Dodge replied as he got up.

"Not so fast," Lemkie said as he looked at Dodge. "You mentioned you had something to tell me about the prints on the laptop."

"Oh, right."

Dodge left the room and returned a moment later with an empty whiskey bottle in a plastic bag. He placed this on the desk as he spoke. "I just want to eliminate any possibility that I'm wrong on this one before I say anything else. Run the prints on this and let me know what you find."

"Panty Bandit fingerprints?" Lemkie asked.

Dodge shrugged. "You tell me."

"What's with the paper in the bottle?" Lemkie asked.

"If the prints do belong to the Panty Bandit, and only then, read the note," Dodge replied. "This will tell you who killed Colonel Mustard in the library with the lead pipe."

Lemkie shook his head, as he didn't have a clue what Dodge was rambling about, but he assumed that he was telling him the note would reveal the identity of the Panty Bandit.

58

The large black feline named Odessa purred and rubbed itself on Mavis' leg as the old woman stood transfixed on the small covered porch of her modest little house. Mavis had a cordless phone pressed against her ear as she watched the commotion unfold next door through her thick glasses. In the driveway of the small bungalow, with the perfectly manicured cedar bushes, were a red sports car, a truck, and now a white car, which must have arrived without Mavis noticing. Mavis had no idea what kinds they were, only that the red one was snazzy, the truck big, and the white one looked practical, she had said to Emma who was on the other end of the phone.

The little house had been put up for sale with Red Realty. She had found this out a week prior from that nice man named Dave who put up the sign. Mavis had bribed the nice man with homemade raisin cookies. Afterwards, Emma had told her that Dave was the man rumoured to be sleeping with Vernon. But today, Mavis had heard screaming and had been afraid to go outside and see what it was about. Instead she called her friend Emma, who quickly insisted that she have some balls and go outside; how else was Mavis going to tell Emma everything that was going on next door. Reluctantly, Mavis went and now she stood on her porch, cordless phone to her ear as she spoke to her friend.

"Admit it, you cheating bitch!" Trudy Wilkins shouted.

A large man in a Hawaiian shirt stood on the stone walkway between her and the porch where Marci Grant stood.

"Whoa, lady, calm down," the man said.

Marci Grant stood on the covered porch with a short round woman, who looked frightened and uncomfortable.

"Go home, Trudy," Marci said. "We'll talk when I get home."

"You're going to deny it to my face, aren't you?" Trudy

shouted as she tried to get past the big man and halfway succeeded. The large man spun around and grasped Trudy, wrapping his large hands around her upper arms. She struggled to lurch forward but he held her in place with very little effort.

"Calm down, lady," he said.

Mavis, while still on her porch, reported to Emma what she was seeing.

"The crazy blonde woman," Emma said in reply. "She's that lesbian lawyer. She and the real-estate lady, Marci, are lovers."

"I wish I was young again," Mavis said into the phone. "That Marci Grant woman is hot."

For a moment Emma went silent, shocked at first, but then laughed. Emma had just learned something new about her friend but would forget about it again, with all the excitement. She would only recall it months later at a Naughty Knitters meeting.

"You were fucking him, weren't you?" Trudy shouted at Marci.

"What are you talking about?" Marci asked.

"That asshole, Charlie!" Trudy replied.

"Are you kidding me??" Marci shouted, as the short round woman next to her shrank and took a step back in fear.

"Lady, I don't want to hurt you," the big man said.

"I don't care how big his dick was," Marci said, who was cut off before she could continue.

"Then why were you going to see him?" Trudy asked, who had stopped struggling against the big man's grip.

"He was gonna buy a house," Marci replied. "I sell houses, remember that?"

"You were fucking him," Trudy replied. "I know his type all too well."

"I sell houses, which is something you should know because that's how we met. Look, Trudy, this jealousy has got to stop," Marci said, her voice raised in anger.

"I love you and this is how you treat me," Trudy replied, who tried unsuccessfully to yank one of her arms free. She glanced back at the large man who was starting to sweat. "Let me go!" she said firmly, as if it was a last warning.

"If you calm down, sure," the large man said, in a calm, soothing voice.

"I've never cheated on you," Marci replied. "Lord knows I could have, but I didn't."

"Fuck you!" Trudy shouted. "Why don't you love me like I love you?"

Mavis reported back to Emma, who was standing on her own porch now, agitated and asking what was happening.

"Tell me!" Emma barked at Mavis, who was doing her best to fill her in on all the juicy gossip.

"Oh, they must be hot in the sack, those two," Mavis blurted before she realized what she had said.

"What's happening?" Emma replied frantically. "Oh, you need to get one of those fancy phones that takes video."

Mavis filled her in on how the large man held the crazy blonde back so she wouldn't kill the sexy redhead. Mavis told Emma other neighbours were watching, too, now. Emma muttered a few curses at this, since now the gossip would spread too fast.

"Loving you isn't enough for you," Marci replied. "And I'm sorry if I'm not dead and notice other women."

"If you really did love me like you say you do, then I'd be enough for you," Trudy replied as she began struggling against the large man again.

"I can't do this anymore," Marci replied. "You need help!"

"What? How dare you say that I...I need help, you fucking horny cunt!" Trudy shouted as she fiercely tugged at the big man's grasp.

"Miss Grant," the large man said. "I think you better go inside. You, too, honey," he said to his wife.

Trudy leaned forward, tugging against the big man's grip as she stomped her fancy three-inch heel down on the top of his foot. The man screamed in pain and his grip on Trudy's arms began to slip.

"Oh fuck!" Mavis exclaimed to Emma. "She done did it now, that crazy bitch."

"What? What'd she do?" Emma asked exuberantly.

Mavis explained how Trudy had stomped on the big man. Her explanations were rushed and garbled as the excitement got the better of her. The big man looked like he was hurting, Mavis relayed to Emma.

Marci took a step back and rushed through the front door of the bungalow, quickly followed by the short round woman who was huffing, out of breath from the exertion. Marci shut the screen door and locked it before closing the ornate solid wooden door behind it and locking it, too. She turned to see the short round woman had dug out what she assumed was an asthma pump and was wheezing between puffs.

Trudy lifted her foot, readying herself to stomp again, when the big man chose to release the crazy little blonde woman.

"Oh shit," Mavis blurted to Emma. "He let her go."

"Who?" Emma asked.

"The big man in the Hawaiian shirt," Mavis replied. "Shit's gonna get realistic now. That's what the kids say," Mavis blurted.

Odessa moved from between the old lady's feet, narrowly avoiding being stepped on in the excitement. The black cat hopped up onto the wide wood railing of the porch and sat before Mavis, who absentmindedly petted her as she excitedly regaled Emma with the events as they unfolded.

"I think everyone in town has lost their minds," Mavis said to Emma.

"Oh, you don't know the half of it," Emma blurted.

"You and your patient confidentiality bullshit," Mavis replied. "You love rubbing it in that you have all these juicy stories you say you won't tell the Naughty Knitters."

"What's happening now?" Emma asked, deflecting Mavis's rant about her keeping all the best gossip to herself.

Trudy turned to face the man, expecting him to be coming at her, to grab her again. Instead she watched as he raised his hands up, palms out in a gesture of surrender. The pained expression on his face and limp said he was still getting over the crushing heel to the top of his foot. Trudy climbed the few steps to the porch, stomping her feet as she did.

"Come out here, you bitch!" Trudy shouted.

Marci and the short round woman backed away from the door.

The large man in the Hawaiian shirt staggered slightly and pulled out a cell phone from his pocket. He gasped for air as beads of sweat ran down his face. He dialled 911 as he put his free hand on his chest and the phone to his ear.

"Small bungalow on Peach Street," he said as soon as the operator had picked up.

Trudy tried opening the screen door but it was locked. She looked around the porch, unsure of what to do next. In a frantic move she picked up the cheap metal-and-canvas chair that was on the small covered porch and bashed at the screen door with the chair legs. The glass resonated but took the blow. She hit it a second time as she shouted.

"Get out here, you bitch! Talk to me!"

Odessa, frightened by the bashing on the door, dropped off the railing and quickly entered the house through a cat door and found one of her favourite hiding places while Mavis watched on, relating all the details to Emma.

The large man in the Hawaiian shirt grasped his chest harder, closing his eyes tight to try and stop the sweat from running into his eyes and blinding him as he spoke.

"Peach Street," he repeated as he struggled to remember

the house number. "I'm having a heart attack and some crazy bitch is trying to kill our real-estate agent." He then proceeded to drop to his knees before falling forward; he lay half on the sidewalk and half on the lawn.

"Oh, fuck!" Mavis blurted to Emma. "I think he's dead."

"Who?" Emma shouted in frustration. "Who's dead?"

"The man in the Hawaiian shirt; he grabbed his chest and fell over face first," Mavis added. "I think I need to hang up and call 911."

"Don't you frickin dare, you old witch!" Emma exclaimed. "You tell me what's going on."

And Mavis did just that.

Trudy broke the glass of the screen door on her fifth attempt and then began bashing at the solid interior door as both Marci and the short round woman grasped at each other in fear.

Mavis noticed that a few other neighbours now were taking videos as she updated Emma. Moments later a police cruiser arrived, followed by an ambulance. The paramedics tended to the large man as the young uniformed officer drew his Taser and radioed for backup.

Mavis couldn't see as well now from this vantage point and had to argue with Emma, who wanted Mavis to get closer to get a better look. Mavis reminded Emma that she was an old woman and could get hurt, although Emma seemed more concerned with not missing a bit of the action. Mavis moved enough to get a better look but refused to get off her own porch.

Trudy took a step back from the door, oblivious to what was happening behind her as she decided the battered chair was no match for the solid wooden door. Instead she decided to attack the window a few feet away from the door. She never did hear the young officer as he hollered for her to *show me your hands* as he came up behind her. As she swung the chair back, readying to strike the window, the chair back struck the officer in the face, breaking his nose and causing his grip to tighten on the trigger on his Taser, shooting Trudy, the twin darts hitting her on the lower back and buttocks. The shock was too late to stop Trudy, as she had already flung the chair into the window, breaking it and sending shards of glass flying into the house, cutting up the window's sheer curtain in the process. Trudy convulsed from the shock of the Taser as the officer grasped at his face with his free hand, jolts of pain shooting through the officer's head as tears filled his eyes. He staggered backwards and fell off the porch, toppling over a stair rail and landing in one of the perfectly manicured cedar bushes. During his fall backwards he had released the Taser to try and grasp at something. With the Taser trigger now released, Trudy collapsed on the floor of the covered porch and twitched from the after-effects.

Now Mavis stood speechless on her own porch, her thick glasses having slipped to the tip of her nose as Emma was frantically asking her what was going on, over and over.

"Mavis?" Emma said. "You there? Ester's the deaf one, not you... Hello?"

In that moment, Mavis accidentally hung up on Emma when she fumbled the phone. Moments later, the phone rang with a frantic Emma on the other end of the call, demanding to know what was going on.

Only after the commotion next door had completely calmed did Odessa eventually reappear from hiding and leave through the cat door, the same way she had come not so long ago.

"Tell me the part where he shot her again," Emma said as she giggled.

"He used one of them Tasers," Mavis replied. "Oh, Lord, that was funny, now that I think about it."

Both ladies burst into fits of giggles just as Mavis accidentally hung up on Emma again. This time Mavis would call Emma back and it would take her the better part of an hour to recap what she had seen unfold next door to her modest little home.

59

"Did you hear?" Lemkie asked as he dropped into the chair across from Detective Dodge's desk. While sitting in front of Dodge, he pivoted the chair to face Detective Tilley who sat at her own desk.

"Okay, I'll bite," Dodge said. "Hear what?"

"Sam called from Elder's Funeral Parlor and claimed the body," Lemkie replied.

"Vernon's?" Tilley asked.

"Charlie Baker's" Lemkie replied.

"I don't get it," Dodge replied.

"Me neither," Tilley replied.

"You love doing this, don't you?" Dodge asked, referring to how Lemkie always stretched out conversations when he had something new to tell them.

Lemkie smirked as he continued updating the pair of detectives. "Apparently Charlie has a daughter."

"A what?" Dodge replied in shock as he looked at Tilley. "Did you know about this?"

"Nope," Tilley replied.

"Apparently, according to Sam, she found out from her mother, who only heard about it all because of the Lucy Shaffer tabloid news about the videos of her and the late Charlie Baker." Lemkie smiled as he saw the looks of confusion on the detectives' faces. "Anyway, that's not important. What is important is that she claimed the body and made the arrangements for a funeral."

"A funeral, here… in Poplar Falls?" Tilley asked.

"Well, she hired Sam to take care of it all," Lemkie replied. "Apparently, the mother and Charlie were never really a thing, so she couldn't do it, but his daughter is the only family he had who came forward to claim the remains."

"But the funeral will be here in Poplar Falls?" Tilley asked a second time.

"Apparently so," Lemkie replied. "Sam said she didn't ask too many questions. He said he had to convince her to give him a wake, for his friends here in town. She eventually agreed to it and said to give him a simple wake plus funeral and to send her the bill."

"Send her the bill," Tilley said. "I assume that means she won't be there?"

"From what I understood, I doubt it," Lemkie replied.

"I doubt they were very close," Dodge added. "It's not like Charlie Baker was the nicest guy."

"I suppose, but..." Lemkie stated.

"Chances are, if her mother was just a fling like the rest of the women in Charlie Baker's life, she might not be that fond of her father," Dodge said.

"True," Lemkie replied. "I sorta wonder who the mother is."

"Me, too," Dodge replied.

"Well, it's not really that important," Tilley replied. "Since we know who killed Charlie now."

"Speaking of which," Lemkie replied. "When are you guys picking her up?"

"I take it *you* didn't hear," Dodge stated with a smirk as he glanced at Tilley. Now he had something that Lemkie didn't know and found the idea of drawing it out very amusing.

Tilley frowned at them both, as she disapproved of the game they played. "She was picked up late yesterday for a domestic disturbance."

The detectives could see the look of confusion on Lemkie's face as they explained further.

"After we watched the video with you, we sent officers to

her office downtown to make sure to pick her up before she could fly off to Mexico or something, but she wasn't there," Dodge said. "Turns out she was on Peach Street with Marci Grant."

"Losing her shit," Tilley added. "She went to Peach Street to see Marci, gave her client a heart attack while she went crazy."

"How do you give someone a heart attack?" Lemkie asked.

"Those were the paramedic's words, not mine," Tilley replied.

"So, let me get this straight," Lemkie said. "We've got Trudy Wilkins in custody for the murder of Charlie Baker. Plus, we've got Sadie Cross in custody for killing her husband, Vernon Cross. Both in holding cells right this minute?"

"Yes and no," Tilley replied. "Trudy is here, yes, but still being held on the domestic disturbance charge. We were letting her cool her heels before charging her on the Charlie Baker murder. Sadie Cross is still at the hospital. When she woke up, strapped to a bed at the hospital, she freaked out, went crazy. She was screaming, asking who was going to watch her kids while she went to murder her husband. She tore open the stitches on her arm and became completely hysterical when she saw her own blood."

"Wow," Lemkie replied.

"So, they're holding her at the hospital. At least until she's somewhat back to normal, and then we'll bring her in," Tilley added.

"What a crazy week this is turning out to be," Lemkie stated.

"Speaking of crazy," Dodge said. "Did you get around to asking Calvin about the hacked Lucy Shaffer videos?"

"Hell no," Lemkie replied, rolling his eyes. "Sadie killing her husband sort of kept us a little busy."

"Speaking of busy, did you run those prints for me yet?"

Dodge asked.

"Not yet. Blame Sadie, she's the one who picked a bad time to kill her husband," Lemkie replied. Dodge gave him a look, so he added, "I'm going to run them this morning; unless someone else gets murdered, that is."

60

It was close to ten in the morning and Detective Franklin Dodge stood in front of Walter's shed, waiting for the firefighters to give him the all-clear to go into the trailer where Walter lived. Earlier that morning, a passing motorist had noticed smoke billowing from the old trailer and had immediately called 911.

The sun shone into the shed enough for Dodge not to need his pocket flashlight to see the adult-sized tricycle, complete with two wire baskets (front and back). And still hooked to the rear was a small empty trailer cart. This looked odd to Dodge and he wasn't sure why at first until he realized he was used to seeing it full of bottles and cans. Dodge finally got to see where the simple young man stored it when he wasn't on his usual route; in this dilapidated shed with the permanently wedged-open door which was half torn off its hinges. Dodge could see enough of the shed to see it was a mess now, but it had probably been organized at some point. Certain things in the back of the shed were neatly stacked, but the rest of it was strewn about in a weird chaotic order that he assumed would have made sense to someone like Walter.

Dodge checked his Blackberry, but still no missed calls or texts from his partner. He assumed she was probably getting coffee or on her way back to the station. She'd call him back he thought as he watched a firefighter carrying an axe exit the house. There hadn't been any smoke when Dodge arrived on the scene, as it had already been contained. The firefighters had gotten there just in time to prevent it from turning into a major fire, they had told him. A frayed wire had started smouldering with some plastics melting and had been on the verge of setting the entire place ablaze.

The fire chief, a short stocky firefighter with a huge mustache, leaned out the door and waved Dodge over. He spoke in a low, growling voice when Dodge approached.

"You need to see this," the fire chief said.

The first thing Dodge noticed was the powerful smell of smoke, garbage, and old sweat. The smell was bad and made him gag as he followed the fire chief. There was garbage strewn about and a path of dirty floor leading straight to the kitchen. Dodge was amazed at the chaos he saw everywhere. After everything he had heard about Walter's mother, there was no way she would live like this. They walked past a cluttered freezer. On top of the freezer Dodge noticed a scattered pile of papers and junk mail, most of which was unopened. Amidst this was an out of place large, battered box filled with crumpled bills and change. At a glance there looked to be hundreds of dollars in the box, if not more. Walking past the freezer he noticed about half of the kitchen drawers and cupboards were open and looked like they had been that way a long time. Old dishes were strewn about, as well as empty cans of assorted stews. An old trouble light with a smoky burnt bulb hung off a blackened cupboard door. Its wire disappeared under a pile of strewn melted plastic dishes and blackened trash. The area around it looked less blackened, and there were more melted plastic dishes as well. He assumed the light had been the source of the smoke. The fire chief would later confirm his suspicions, as the wire from the old trouble light was badly frayed in some places.

The fire chief stopped at a doorway and indicated for Dodge to look inside. As Dodge looked into the bedroom, he understood what the stocky mustached man had wanted him to see. In the filthy bed lay the contorted body of a scrawny Walter.

"Smoke inhalation," the fire chief said. "I assume it smouldered a long time before someone noticed and called us."

Dodge's Blackberry rang. He dug it out to see the call was coming from the station. The fire chief walked away as Dodge entered the bedroom while answering the call.

"Hey," Dodge said, expecting to hear Tilley on the other end of the call but was surprised when it wasn't.

"I just read the note in that whiskey bottle," Lemkie said. "Are you serious?"

"Dead serious," Dodge replied as he looked at the body before him.

"Who else have you told?" Lemkie asked.

"Just Tilley," Dodge replied as he stood looking at the scrawny young man. His face was contorted as if he had struggled for breath in the end. "I needed to be sure."

"Well, if the prints on the bottle were his, you can be certain now."

"Have you seen Tilley?" Dodge asked as he looked around the room and marvelled at the clutter. He pulled his pocket flashlight out and scanned around as he spoke. "I tried calling her but she didn't pick up."

"You going to arrest Walter?" Lemkie asked. "I mean, I know he's brain-damaged now but, you can't not, can you?"

"Now you understand why I wanted to be sure," Dodge replied as he shone his flashlight into the closet and saw an open cardboard box with purple lacy fabric protruding from it. He peered into the box and saw the proof he needed to solidify this to everyone else.

"Find anything interesting?" he heard the low, growling voice say from behind him. He turned to see the fire chief standing directly behind him.

Dodge pointed to the box and stepped out of the way so

the fire chief could see for himself. As the short, stocky man looked inside the box, Dodge continued his phone conversation.

"Well, my decisions already been made for me," Dodge replied.

"I'll be a monkey's uncle," the fire chief said as he stepped back and looked at Dodge. "Is that what I think it is?"

"What do you mean by that?" Lemkie asked. "I mean, we got him, right?"

"Yeah," Dodge replied to both Lemkie and the fire chief as he turned his attention to the body in the bed. In that moment he felt pity for the young man, even if he knew he shouldn't. Had he been looking at the old Walter, the young man who frightened all the women of Poplar Falls, he would have felt numb to the young man. Many years of seeing senseless crimes had hardened him to feel no empathy towards people like Walter; although he had gotten to know the new Walter. The simple-minded young man who had a one-track mind and never hurt anyone was different than who he had been previously. Dodge recalled going to homes that had been broken in to and seeing the devastation on the women's faces. They felt violated. No longer safe in their own homes. The old Walter had taken that from them as well as the lacy material he so badly desired. He couldn't help but think this was karma coming to visit Walter to enact its own brand of cruel revenge on the deserving young man. And after the deaths of Charlie Baker and now Walter, it looked like karma had taken up residence in Poplar Falls.

"Dodge, you still there?" Lemkie asked.

"Just a sec," Dodge said to Lemkie as he turned to the fire chief, who was walking out of the bedroom with his head down in disgust. "Chief," Dodge called out. "Can you keep this quiet until we can get this scene locked down?"

"Fuckin' sicko bastard," the fire chief grumbled through his thick mustache. "Yeah, I'll keep this quiet."

Although the other firemen had already fed the rumour mill about Walter being dead, none of them knew the fact that he was also the Panty Bandit.

"Walter's dead, Lemkie. And we found the proof we need to close the Panty Bandit case once and for all," Dodge said. "How fast can you get to Walter's house?"

"I'll grab my stuff and leave as soon as I can," Lemkie replied. "Should I bring Calvin?"

"If you still trust him then you might want to, as this place is a mess."

"Worse than Charlie Baker's?"

"Big time," Dodge replied.

"I still trust him to do his job," Lemkie replied. "I'll bring him along and we'll see from there."

"And tell Tilley to come, too," Dodge replied before ending the call and exiting the bedroom. He walked out to find the fire chief waiting for him by the front door as he did.

"Those," the fire chief growled as he pointed to a pair of yellow wires that ran through a hole in the wall next to the front door of the trailer. "Those go to the neighbour's house."

"Those?" Dodge asked.

"The electricity is off in the place. Walter must have run these from the neighbour's. One of my guys disconnected them to make sure the place wouldn't burn down still."

Dodge thought this was a wild idea, as the Walter he knew wouldn't have the smarts to do this sort of rigging. But what Dodge didn't know was that Walter used to have good days when he could figure these things out. But those days had faded away as time passed and simple tasks got harder for Walter. Things like paying electric bills were a thing of the past for Walter, let alone figuring out how to get power from an unsuspecting neighbour.

Dodge looked around and noted the trouble light hanging from the kitchen cabinet. There was another trouble light hanging from an old hook in the ceiling near the bedroom door. This one looked like it might still work if it had power, thought Dodge. And in the stillness of the place, Dodge heard no white noise at all in the old trailer. That's when he noticed the white freezer with the clutter of papers on top of its lid. He took out his Blackberry and took a couple of pictures of the top of the freezer and its cluttered mess. He pocketed the phone, took the box from the top of the freezer, and swept the papers and unopened mail into it. Dodge set the box of money and papers on the floor next to him and put his hand on the freezer, feeling warmth from the compressor which indicated it still had power until recently, when the fireman had disconnected the extension cords. The yellow wire he now saw running behind must be for this freezer and this made him nervous. He steeled himself and opened the freezer lid, bracing for what he would find.

Inside, still frozen and covered in frost, was exactly what Dodge knew he would find: the body of Walter's mother. Although he had half expected to find her chopped up or something like in the movies, he was surprised to see she looked to be completely intact. And it was hard to tell with the frost, but the expression on her face even had a serene look to it. Not the horrified expression he had expected to find.

"Jesus Christ," he heard the growling voice of the fire chief exclaim as he turned to see him standing next to him. "What a sick fuck that kid was."

Dodge marvelled at everything he had just learned about simple Walter. Not only was he the Panty Bandit, but he had probably killed his own mother and stuffed her into a freezer. But he couldn't get past the look on the old woman's face. She didn't look like someone who died fighting off her simple son. She looked peaceful in a strange sort of way.

"Maybe we should plug this back up until my crime scene guy comes in," Dodge said to the fire chief. "I'm not sure how he's going to want to handle this one."

"Sick fuck," the fire chief said as he walked out of the

trailer.

Dodge gently closed the lid of the freezer. "Damn," he whispered to himself as he heard the compressor of the freezer come to life while it contained nothing but death inside it. Dodge looked at the box of paper next to him. He noticed many of the papers in the box looked identical. Each one looked like it had been left outside for a week before being put in this box. Each copy looked like it had gotten wet and rubbed in dirt before being left here in the pile. Dodge carefully plucked one of the identical papers from the box and unfolded it, reading the text on the top.

Elder's Funeral Parlor.

There must have been thirty copies of this, maybe more in the box with the money. They had been scattered on the lid of the freezer before being put in the box just now by the curious detective. The money, thought Dodge, must have been to pay for his mother's funeral. The peaceful look on her face told Dodge what the coroner would later confirm. Walter's mother died peacefully, probably in her sleep would be his best guess. Her heart just stopped, leaving Walter to fend for himself. Something he could have done before his operation, but not since. His physical condition was evidence enough, but one look at the place and you knew that he had been declining in ability for a long time. Perhaps the brain tumour was back or perhaps they just took too much when they saved this poor wretched young man's life; the same young man who now lay dead from smoke inhalation in his own bed. Although, to look at his condition, it was only a matter of time before he'd have died of malnutrition or dehydration.

Dodge now stood at the bedroom door, looking at the body in the bed, trying to remind himself that this was the young man who terrorized the women of Poplar Falls. Dodge felt sorry for him, and yet another part of him couldn't help but think it was some form of twisted poetic justice for the young man to have suffered so much.

"I didn't believe you when you told me the place was worse than Charlie Baker's, but I do now," Lemkie said as he walked into the trailer, Detective Tilley in tow. They walked over to where Dodge stood by the bedroom door and peered inside.

"I don't mean to sound insensitive," Tilley said, "but karma seems to be doing a good chunk of our job for us."

Dodge didn't vocalize a response to Tilley's statement, as it did ring a little sour. But that didn't change the fact that he fully agreed with her, at least in this case he thought. Not so in the case of Vernon Cross, though. Vernon might not have been the best of people, but he certainly hadn't deserved to be stabbed to death with a wooden dick.

"You mentioned having proof that could close the Panty Bandit case?" Lemkie asked.

"In the closet there's a box full of evidence. But that's not the worse part," Dodge said as he took Tilley and Lemkie over to the freezer.

"What now?" Lemkie lamented, who really didn't want to know but it was his job to find out.

Dodge opened the freezer while a speechless Lemkie peered inside. Dodge handed the funeral parlour brochure to Tilley. She looked at the brochure and quickly pieced it together. The box of money containing many more identical copies of the pamphlet was all the clues she needed. Walter was saving up to bury his mother. The young man she was beginning to see as some sort of perverted monster had been part human after all. Feeling sick to her stomach from a combination of what she was seeing and smelling, Tilley dropped the brochure in the box and went outside to get fresh air.

61

The night air was warm and muggy again, just like it had been for the last week, which was the perfect weather to breed mosquitoes. The two detectives sat in Dodge's screened-in porch, enjoying the quiet night air, the only sounds being the frustrated mosquitoes on the screens in search of a way inside. Dodge, still in his running shorts and T-shirt, smelled of sweat but he didn't care. Neither did Tilley, even though she showered at the gym before heading home. But before going inside her home, she crossed the street to sip beer in Dodge's porch.

"Well, the coroner confirmed my suspicions," Dodge said. "Walter's mother died of heart failure. Died in her sleep, he figured. She was already long dead when Walter put her in the freezer."

"I know he wasn't right in the head anymore..."

"Anymore? I don't think he was ever right in the head," Dodge said.

"I just wonder why he wouldn't call an ambulance... or us. Why wouldn't he have called the cops? His mother was dead."

"I don't think he was able to think it through like a normal person anymore," Dodge replied.

Tilley sipped her beer before responding. "Rumours are spreading like wildfire that Walter was the Panty Bandit."

"Well, considering that the break-ins stopped when he had his surgery, it won't take long now for people to talk up a storm. Besides, isn't the fire chief Geraldine's neighbour?"

"Yeah," Tilley replied. "She'll be plying him for information, that's for sure."

"I bumped into Ester at the Food Emporium," Dodge replied.

"I bet she wanted to know if the penis cozy fit," Tilley replied with a chuckle.

She did actually ask that very question, thought Dodge. But he wouldn't give Tilley the chance to laugh at him with this one. Dodge ignored the comment and continued. "She wanted to know about Walter and his mom, if the rumours were true."

"Well, if the Naughty Knitters are talking about it, there's no stopping the rumour mill. Not that I assumed we could or anything."

"This town isn't what I expected when I moved here, let me tell you that," Dodge replied before drinking the rest of his beer. He went to his cabinet which hid the mini fridge and got a fresh can of beer and put his empty in its place.

"Speaking of rumours," Tilley added. "I bumped into Marci Grant at the gym earlier tonight."

"How was she? I mean, we arrested her girlfriend for murder, after all. Or did she flirt with you again?" Dodge asked with a smirk as he cracked open his beer.

"Actually, she wasn't her usual self," Tilley replied. She sipped beer and continued. "She was much colder, more serious, and not her usual flirty self."

"So I take that as a no," Dodge said, wondering if that had been disappointment he heard just now in Tilley's voice.

Tilley ignored her partner's comments as she continued. "She asked how Trudy was. She sounded concerned."

"What does that have to do with rumours?" Dodge asked. "You said, speaking of rumours."

"Well, turns out that Dave, the guy Vernon was seeing, is a carpenter and woodworker."

"That explains the intricately carved lamp," Dodge said.

"Yes, that. And turns out he's the one who makes and puts up Marci Grant's real-estate signs."

"This town is getting smaller and smaller all the time," Dodge quipped. "What does that have to do with anything?"

"Well, according to Marci, Vernon was going to leave his wife and come out. So he could be with Dave."

Dodge didn't have a reply for that and sipped beer instead. Tilley finished her beer and got another before Dodge changed the subject.

"Sadie's still in the hospital."

"I knew that," Tilley replied.

"No, I mean she had another episode today," Dodge replied. "Freaked out, tried to bite a nurse and punched the doctor in the face, so they restrained and sedated her again."

"I have to admit I assumed she was faking it, but I'm not sure anymore."

"It must be something in the water to make all you Poplar Falls women crazy," Dodge said.

"Don't you go lumping us all together now," Tilley replied. "We're not all crazy."

"Did Lemkie tell you Calvin gave his notice?"

"What? Are you serious?"

"I'm thinking Lemkie wasn't surprised," Dodge stated. "He thinks Calvin knows that he knows he leaked the Lucy Shaffer sex tapes. But he also knows that Lemkie doesn't have proof. Anyway, Lemkie said he quit because he couldn't handle the stress of it all."

"Bad timing," Tilley replied.

"Well, he's not gone yet," Dodge added. "Said he'd stick around until things settle down for Lemkie."

"Well, between the video and Trudy confessing, that'll settle the Charlie Baker investigation. And there's really nothing to investigate on Walter since he died of smoke inhalation and didn't actually murder his mother."

"True," Dodge replied. "But he still has to process the Sadie Vernon murder, not to mention all the new Panty Bandit evidence."

"And here I was, hoping for a quiet summer," Tilley stated, sipping beer.

"You going to Charlie Baker's wake tomorrow?"

"Why?" Tilley asked. "Why would I go to that?"

"I don't know about you, but I'm curious to see who goes and who doesn't."

"After everything that happened, I do have to admit to being a bit curious," Tilley replied with a smile. "But you're probably just going to see if Ms. Weatherbee will be there."

"Very funny," Dodge replied.

Tilley guffawed. "It wouldn't kill you to date. I don't think I've seen you date since you moved here."

"Life is easier that way," Dodge replied. "Nobody disappoints you, or you them. When you're alone, nobody betrays you or shuns your affections. Plus, we live in a trade-up society. Most people in relationships are always looking for better. Bah... Besides, I'm old and set in my ways." Dodge purposely left out the part where he had felt trapped in the last few years of his marriage and was enjoying freedom too much to want to change that. Tilley didn't need to hear that part, he thought.

"You can't just give up," Tilley replied.

"I never said I gave up," Dodge replied with a smile. "When the right woman comes along." Dodge lifted his beer as if to toast and drank.

Tilley finished her beer, got up, and handed her empty to Dodge. "Well, I'm off to get some sleep."

Dodge watched his partner cross the street and disappear into her home. He gathered the empty beer cans and bagged them. Tying the bag shut he set it aside, thinking it wasn't full enough yet to give to Walter. He'd put the bag out on collection day, full or not, he thought as he walked to the washroom to urinate. In mid-stream, he remembered Walter's body lying in bed.

"Shit," he exclaimed as the reality set in that there would be no Walter collection day, ever again.

62

Floral arrangements overpowered the area near the closed casket at Elder's Funeral Parlor. At the Charlie Baker wake Dodge stood in the back of the room, eating a crust-free finger sandwich. It was some sort of sweet-tasting mystery meat he had yet to identify. He ate the dry sandwich while watching the crowd mingle. Many of the people he recognized from the investigation or around town, although there were some men mingling who he didn't recognize. But part of him knew that some of these men were there to see who Charlie Baker's lovers were. Most likely some of them thought that if these women were horny enough to be with Charlie then they might have a shot. Most predatory men like these never included loneliness into the equation. They never realized that most of these women didn't like Charlie Baker for his sexual prowess or the size of his manhood, but rather how he made them feel about themselves. From what he gathered, Charlie Baker had a way of making the women feel desired and interesting. That's what they wanted. At least that's what Dodge assumed they wanted. He was no expert when it came to women. Sure, they thought he was handsome, but charming wasn't a word most women used to describe him.

Ham, he wondered to himself as he swallowed, wishing he had something to wash it down with. It must be ham in these sandwiches, with some sort of spice or sauce.

63

Across the room, Emma and her cronies each sat with a plate as they watched people mingle at the wake and gossiped. Each of them had their bag of knitting supplies, as the women would need to have a Naughty Knitters meeting afterwards.

"Look at all these women," Emma said to the other ladies. "Charlie Baker was charming, but I didn't think he was that good."

"He must have been crazy to be seeing all those women at the same time," Agatha said. "Women are jealous by nature. One of them was bound to kill him eventually."

"You were seeing him, too," Mavis quipped with a smile and a wink. Everyone knew Mavis was referring to the peephole Agatha had used to watch Charlie having sex.

Agatha blushed fiercely and gave Mavis the stink eye. She would never live this one down, but on the bright side, as a result of everything, Myrtle had shown her some of the best websites for pornography.

"I don't understand what all the fuss is about," Geraldine said. "There is such a thing as too big, you know."

"What?" Ester asked.

"Oh, for God's sake, someone turn up Ester's hearing aid," Emma said as she adjusted her bag of knitting supplies.

"They should have put up a picture of his Johnson," Mavis said with a smile. She was referring to the picture next to the closed casket. No one really knew who it came from, but one of the ladies had provided a picture of a smiling Charlie Baker. "More would have recognized him with a picture of his Johnson."

"Mavis!" Geraldine scolded.

"What?" Mavis replied with a smile and wink.

"My George says not all men want a lot of women," Geraldine said, wife of Pastor George. "Some are happy with just one."

"Men are pigs," Emma blurted.

"Emma!" Geraldine scolded.

"Well, it's the truth. If you want it sugar-coated, get a donut," Emma replied.

"What?" Ester asked.

"I went with Ester to her doctor's appointment last week," Geraldine said. "He told her she had Celiac disease. She thought he said she had silly ass disease."

All the women except for Ester laughed, garnering disapproving looks from many of the others at the wake.

64

Standing in the funeral parlour, Dodge couldn't help but think about Walter and his brochures. He had accumulated many of them, which Dodge assumed meant he came here often. Perhaps to make the arrangements, but not being able to vocalize what he wanted, like he would have before his surgery, must have been unbelievably frustrating. His mother's body stayed preserved while he tried to make enough money to give her a proper burial. Sam Elder confirmed what Dodge suspected. Walter would come by, take a brochure, and leave. Sometimes he tried to talk to Sam, but with a limited vocabulary, Walter would get flustered and leave. Dodge had Walter on his mind when he spotted Calvin walking over with a plate of mystery meat sandwiches and cheese cubes on toothpicks. Calvin's black eye was barely noticeable now.

"I'm surprised to see you here," Dodge said.

"I thought the guy who jumped me for the list of women might come to the wake," Calvin replied. "I thought there might be a chance I can identify him."

"Good point," Dodge replied, scanning the room for men he didn't know.

"It irks me that he got away with it."

"I hear you gave Lemkie your notice."

"Yup," Calvin replied. "I can't do this anymore. My nerves are shot and it's no secret that I throw up when I'm stressed out too much. I just can't anymore. I'm on anxiety meds, too, now."

"I suppose we're not all cut out for law enforcement," Dodge replied.

"Besides, I got a new job and the benefits are pretty awesome," Calvin said as he ate cheese and stared off in the distance.

Dodge glanced in the direction Calvin was looking and noticed Stella Rubbin, smiling slightly as she returned Calvin's gaze.

65

"Who's that?" Stella asked of no one in particular as she stood near the flower arrangements in Elder's Funeral Parlor.

Marci Grant, who stood nearby, followed Stella's gaze to a short, busty Asian woman who sat alone.

"I don't remember her name, but she looked at the Turlington house a while ago," Marci replied.

Stella looked Marci up and down. She was wearing her usual tight-fitting business attire and her battered brown driving gloves, which Trudy would have given her grief over. Then Stella realized she had actually vocalized her question out loud. She had managed to stay sober for the funeral, but she still wasn't thinking clearly, and would have killed for a drink right at that moment.

Marci gave her a smile and then returned her gaze at the busty Asian woman. "She's a bit high-strung but she's got a nice frickin' rack," Marci said.

"Those have got to be fake," Stella replied.

"Who cares," Marci replied, which got her a look from Stella that said, are you serious.

"When you're jumping up and down on a trampoline, do you care if it's synthetic or real rubber?" Marci asked with a smirk. "I know I don't. And boy, would I love to see those on a trampoline."

"And here I was thinking only men were jerks," Stella Rubbin replied as she turned and walked away.

Marci scanned the crowd in hopes that maybe, just maybe, Lucy Shaffer might come to Charlie Baker's funeral after all.

66

People at the funeral parlour talked about her, yes, but nobody knew who the short, busty Asian woman was. And while many watched her, no one noticed when she stole a single knitting needle from Geraldine's bag of knitting supplies as she walked past. No one said a thing as she calmly walked toward Stella Rubbin, who stood near the closed casket. Stella was wiping away a tear as the short, busty Asian woman stopped and stood next to her.

"Is dat a Chahlie Baka? You fuck Chahlie?"

Stella looked her up and down before speaking. "Oh, hell no!" she blurted as she walked away. "I've had enough crazy for one day."

Before anyone knew what was happening the Asian woman had flung open the casket while screaming.

"You asshoe!" she shouted as she plunged the knitting needle into the late Charlie Baker's chest. "I get these fa you," the Asian woman shouted as she pointed at her chest. "Fie-tousand-dolla each! They heavy, my back hut a lot."

Some shrieked, others gasped in shock as they watched the short, busty Asian woman burst into hysterics.

"You fucka all dees women... you asshoe!"

Sam Elder wasn't a fit man but he wasn't a small man either, so picking up the tiny Asian woman wasn't very difficult. Nor did the small Asian woman put up much of a fight, except to berate him with verbal abuse.

"You put-a me dow," the Asian woman shouted. "Put-a me dow now!"

Everyone watched as Sam Elder paused, threw the big-breasted Asian woman over his shoulder, and carried her away. And while everyone was enthralled by the spectacle that belonged in some sort of offbeat comedic performance, Mavis was peering into the coffin, trying to see if Charlie Baker still had wood.

67

"What'd I miss?" Tilley whispered to Calvin, having just arrived. In that moment everyone was quiet, having just witnessed what they would call the Charlie Baker Funeral Fiasco that would have the town talking for years. There was no way anyone could ever forget this day, especially since the short, busty Asian woman and Sam Elder would eventually get married.

68

A jingle suddenly broke the silence of the wake and sent Myrtle into a frenzied search through her purse. She pulled out a large, pink-rhinestone-encrusted iPhone and tapped away furiously at it until the resonating sound ceased. With arthritic hands, she fumbled the phone for a moment and then smiled at everyone in the funeral parlour.

Ester looked around, scrunched her nose, and smiled as she spoke. "Myrtle just got a booty call," she said to everyone within ear-shot.

Myrtle flushed fiercely while Emma and Mavis giggled like school girls.

December

69

Agatha sat in the soft light of her Christmas tree, which she had put up on the first of December. The gentle red lights cast a warm glow, and the tree made her feel festive while sitting at the kitchen table where she checked her emails on her laptop. Some of the tenants of her apartment building were happy that their elderly landlady had finally caught up with the times. Apparently one of her tenants needed a plumber to check her bathroom sink, as it had a rotten smell emanating from it. Agatha noted it on her list of things to do.

Between setting her pen down and checking her next email, she paused when she heard something. She waited, holding her breath without realizing she wasn't breathing as she listened. Then she heard it, a repetitive thumping noise. She smiled. The young couple who had taken over Charlie Baker's old apartment were at it again. Those kids fucked like rabbits, she thought as she fought off the temptation to peer through the old peephole. Instead she clicked on the link Myrtle had emailed her.

The link titled *Christmas Balls a Ringing* was everything Myrtle said it would be and then some.

"Oh, my," Agatha said, which she followed up with a gasp as she turned up the volume on her computer.

70

It took Sadie a while to get accustomed to prison life. It wasn't quite what you saw in the movies, but it was still no picnic in there. The trick was to make the right friends. Things got a lot easier with the right friends having your back, especially for a small woman like Sadie Cross. Sadie sat on a bench, holding a rolled-up shirt in her lap while in a general population area, her new friends talking all around her while she barely heard a thing. She had a habit of retreating into her own mind and spending as much time as she could there. She'd stare off into the distance, daydreaming about being at the daycare again. Spending time with the kids was something she missed terribly.

Sometimes she dreamed of lying in Charlie Baker's arms, usually after having sex, and that was better than being here with these women. Many of them were manlier than her dead husband had been. Not that Vernon had been a feminine homosexual. He was quite butch, considering. He'd been a handsome, burly man who'd loved her proper in the early days. The crazy part of it was that she missed him. She missed the time they spent together, watching movies or cooking for guests. Vernon had loved to entertain. God, how could she have been so stupid not to know very early on that Vernon was gay.

Sadie unravelled the shirt she had in her lap. From it she took a slab of foil- covered dark chocolate, exposed some of it, and took a generous bite. Her mind still wrapped up in her fantasies, she did this without even realizing she was being watched. She chewed slowly, savouring the chocolate as she thought about Charlie Baker. In her daydream, she felt Charlie tug on her arm as she was falling asleep. She smiled slightly, as she knew he wanted more. He wanted her again, she thought. Twice in one visit was normal for Charlie Baker, the pills made sure of that, but three times was odd she thought, but she smiled a coy little smile just the same. When she felt the tug on her arm again, she broke from her daydream to find Loraine, her six-foot-two butch friend, was trying to get her attention.

"Friend of yours?" Loraine asked as she gestured with a nod in the direction of a pretty blonde woman.

Sadie broke from her trance, still savouring her dark chocolate, and saw a slightly battered Trudy Wilkins standing not far in front of her. Trudy was staring directly at her when they made eye contact.

"You could say that," Sadie replied.

Trudy scanned the other prisoners before approaching, as if she wanted to make sure it was safe.

Sadie could see Trudy had had it rough so far.

Trudy could see that Sadie, while she didn't look happy, looked like she was doing pretty well. Sadie actually looked like she had gained a few pounds.

"Hey," Trudy said in a meek voice, as if afraid of what would happen as a result.

Loraine tugged on Sadie's arm to get her attention but Sadie kept eye contact with Trudy.

"Hey," Sadie replied. "How're you doing?"

Sadie wasn't as meek as Trudy recalled. She had a serious look instead of that fake smile she often wore whenever they bumped into each other in Poplar Falls.

Trudy wasn't as thin as she used to be, thought Sadie. Plus, the side of her face looked like it was recovering nicely, but still showed some slight bruising.

"I see you're better at making friends in here than I am," Trudy said.

"You can be my friend, too, sweet cheeks," Loraine said.

"Eat me, you cow," Trudy replied, surprised at her own sudden boldness.

"Sure," Loraine replied with a smile and roaming eyes. "You want some dark chocolate, too in exchange for some honey, honey?"

"She's good, too," Sadie said with a blank-faced expression, taking another bite of her dark chocolate which Loraine did get her in exchange for sexual favours. Sadie shrugged and patted the seat next to her, inviting Trudy to join them.

Might as well, thought Trudy as she sat. It was better than being pushed around all the time.

71

Lucy Shaffer's first tweet after coming out of her most recent stint in rehab was shared over a million times. It read as follows.

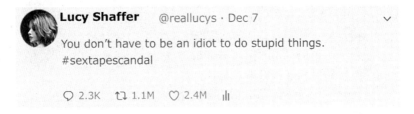

Lucy Shaffer @reallucys · Dec 7 ⌄

You don't have to be an idiot to do stupid things. #sextapescandal

♡ 2.3K ⟲ 1.1M ♡ 2.4M ⬚

The television entertainment shows spoke of an upcoming movie where the comedian would play a woman whose life is forever altered by a sex tape that made its way onto the internet. The script would be loosely inspired by actual events but none of it would resemble anything that happened in Poplar Falls that summer. But the sex tape and the new movie would breathe new life into the career of the sassy comedian. Although her new manager advised against making this new film, Lucy would decide the best way to get past the scandal was to give people something else to talk about.

72

Calvin sat at his desk in his new office in the main building of the Magnolia Wellness and Rehabilitation Centre. The office was small and had no windows, but that was for the best. Fewer distractions that way, and Stella could keep a better eye on her new head of information technology. She had her reasons for wanting to keep him out of trouble and employed as well.

Calvin had moved in with her in the beginning of December, but they didn't tell anyone at the centre, although Emma O'Brien already knew. She had her ways. But this secret she had kept, so far. Emma knew which secrets had to be kept. She also had a way of manipulating rumours when she needed to. That was one advantage of being the unofficial leader of the therapy group who called themselves the Naughty Knitters. Emma also didn't tell anyone about Calvin's new obsession. A dark-skinned busty woman named Stella Rubbin. And Stella had dirt on Calvin, too. She was the only person Calvin ever confessed to about leaking the Lucy Shaffer videos. Calvin hadn't left a trace. The only trace would have been the money, had he gotten paid like he was supposed to. The money was to pay off some bills he was behind on. But being stiffed in a deal like that wasn't exactly something he could go to the cops about. Which had left him stressed out again, but Stella had helped him forget about the money. She had ways of making Calvin forget a lot of things, such as his addiction to pornography.

Calvin hadn't watched any since that day in Stella's office. The day she taught him things about human sexuality that pornography couldn't. Calvin also started to learn how to get past his awkwardness with women. She taught him that women were people, too. Pornography had programmed him to objectify women, and until he met Stella he never realized he did this. And while their relationship had started as purely physical, it had blossomed into more. Neither of them had actually admitted it yet, even to each other, but they each knew it. Stella had a reason to stay sober now and Calvin had no desire to watch pornography. And Charlie Baker had been the reason for it all happening.

73

Emma sat at her kitchen table, wearing her nun's habit, sipping gin. Next to her glass sat her riding crop and next to that was an aerosol can. Mountain Mist deodorant spray. Across from Emma with her own glass of gin sat Myrtle, also wearing a newly acquired nun's habit. Next to her glass was a short-handled whip that was more for show, but still stung pretty good.

"When you suggested a threesome, this is not what I had in mind," Myrtle said as she sipped gin.

"Oh, come on. It'll be fun," Emma replied with a smile as she finished the joint, butted what was left of it out, and took a sip of gin.

"Maybe," Myrtle replied with a smirk. "In a twisted sorta way."

"Well, what other way is there?" Emma said with a smile as she used the aerosol spray to mask the smell of the joint the ladies had shared.

The ladies in their nun's habits laughed and sipped more gin.

"You coming back?" Bill shouted from the basement.

"You shush if you know what's good for you," Emma shouted in reply. "He thinks I'm on the phone again, you watch," Emma said to Myrtle.

"Don't leave me down here for an hour like last time," Bill screamed from the basement, where he waited, bound and helpless. "This wood won't last forever."

"Oh, I'm coming, bad little Billy," Emma said as she sipped the rest of her gin. "Little Billy's been a bad boy, hasn't he? And boy do I have a surprise for little Billy today." Emma smiled and winked at Myrtle.

"Oh, what the hell," Myrtle said, drinking the rest of her gin. "And don't you dare ever mention this at a Naughty Knitters meeting."

The ladies laughed as they went downstairs to surprise Bill, who was waiting where Emma had left him.

74

Marci looked around her home, trying to remember it the way it used to look when Trudy and her daughter still lived with her. The place was always a mess, but it had that lived-in feeling. Now it just felt empty. Trudy's jealousy had been hard to bear but there had always been something special about her. And now there was a void in the house that Marci couldn't shake. Since it was dark out now she flicked the switch, turning on the outdoor Christmas lights Dave had put up for her. She wanted the place to have a welcoming feel to it when people came to see it. Marci had listed it herself and got Dave to put the sign up. She knew she probably shouldn't be doing that, but her price was so low that nobody would accuse her of playing double agent. Not with the deal she'd be giving them. Plus, her new lawyer said he'd help her out with a fellow real-estate agent if she wanted. Help her make the paperwork look more legit, for a small fee of course.

Marci placed a brown-leather-gloved hand on the door-knob, just about to leave as her phone rang. She thought briefly about not answering the call and then remembered how much she needed the money. She dug through her purse and found her phone on the fourth ring.

"Red Realty. Marci Grant speaking."

"Miss Grant. It's Franklin Dodge."

"Detective Franklin Dodge, is this about Trudy?" Marci asked with a wistful tone.

"No-no," Dodge replied. "I'm actually calling you on personal business, to list a house."

"You leaving town?" Marci asked, unsure why this was the first thought that came to her.

"Actually, it's for a friend. She wants to put her house up for sale and I suggested she use you, seeing as how business is down for you with everything that happened and all."

"Well, thank you," Marci replied. "That's very kind of you."

"Actually, the real reason I suggested you is that you're the best in town."

"Now, Dodge, flattery will only get you so far."

"Well, my friend really wants to sell her house."

"No pressure at all," Marci replied with a tone of amusement before continuing. "You know December isn't exactly the best time of year to sell a house."

"Oh, I know that, but we gotta start somewhere," Dodge replied.

"True. Well, I can come by tomorrow morning if your friend is available to go over the details and make arrangements."

"Actually, I was thinking more like tomorrow night, if that's okay. My friend's a teacher and she won't be available in the morning."

"Evening works fine," Marci replied. "I can work with that."

Marci got a pad and pen and took down the address.

"Will you be there tomorrow night, or just your friend?" Marci asked.

"I'm not sure," Dodge replied. He paused for a second then continued. "Yeah, I should be there."

"Seven?"

"Sounds perfect," Dodge replied. "Thank you."

"No, thank you," Marci said as she terminated the call.

75

Dodge hung up the cordless phone, shifted into a comfortable spot on the couch, and put his feet up on the coffee table as he watched the Christmas tree fade from red to clear. Then it faded again to multicoloured and then back to red and so on.

"I should really head home."

Margaret Weatherbee joined him on the couch. "Why not stay the night?" she asked as she snuggled up next to him, grabbing his arm and putting it around her.

Dodge smiled and tightened his grip a bit, hugging her against him for a moment before relaxing. "Maybe I should, but…"

"If you're still worried about people finding out we're seeing each other, then go. But we won't be able to hide it once we move in together, and you know it."

Dodge laughed.

"And you know we're not the only ones with something to hide, right?"

"Yup," Dodge replied.

"I know we've not been dating that long, but we're grown-ups and can do whatever we please."

"Yup."

"And we please," Margaret said with a smile.

"I'm thinking I should sell my house, too," Dodge replied. "We could get a new place together and have more privacy that way."

"Nah," Weatherbee replied. "I like your place. Mind you, it's in severe need of a woman's touch, but I like it."

Dodge hugged her close and they sat quietly for a good while, watching the Christmas tree change colors, bathing the room in the soft glow of the holidays. The quiet lasted a good while until she spoke. "What are you thinking about?"

"I was just thinking that if it wasn't for Charlie Baker moving to Poplar Falls, I probably would have never met you."

"Oh, you," Weatherbee said, playfully swatting at Dodge.

"I certainly wouldn't have gotten that show I got that day outside Charlie's apartment."

"You little brat," she said as she sat up to give him the stink eye. "Did you bring it like I asked?"

Dodge reached into his pocket and fished out something that looked like an oddly shaped mitten.

"And you never tried it on?" referring to the penis cozy given to him by Ester.

"Hell no," Dodge replied with a laugh.

"Well, I want to know if it fits," Weatherbee replied with a wide smile. "Bedroom... now!"

76

Detective Roxanne Tilley sat at her desk, warming her cold hands on a large steaming coffee mug. She leaned back in her chair, propped her feet up on her desk, and closed her eyes. She breathed deeply, savouring the rich coffee aroma as she enjoyed the rare quiet of the Poplar Falls police station bullpen. This December had felt subdued so far and life felt a little normal again, but there was always something going on. So staying late to get caught up on paperwork wasn't an everyday thing, but sometimes it was necessary. But things were pretty quiet, and after last summer that quiet was something Tilley didn't feel would happen again for a long time. But here she was, enjoying a hot cup of coffee, her paperwork almost caught up. She glanced at the clock and knew she had a bit of time to kill. Dodge didn't think his partner knew about his new relationship, but she was a detective after all. And Tilley also knew that the new couple was meeting Red Realty that night to list her former teacher's house. She knew because Marci wasn't good at keeping secrets from her.

With her eyes still closed, Tilley's mind relived the previous evening. She remembered what Marci's gloved hands had felt like on the small of her back. How her kisses had tasted. And each time they were together, their passion melted away all the confusion she had ever experienced throughout her life. Being with Marci confirmed what she always knew but spent most of her life being in denial about.

Still leaning back in her chair, Tilley sipped coffee and woke her computer from its sleep mode. She moused her way to an old folder and clicked on the video she had watched a few dozen times, perhaps more.

Tilley watched the blonde woman, her back to the camera as she kissed the naked Charlie Baker passionately while he gently removed her blouse, leaving her with just matching panties and bra. The blonde woman pushed the clearly aroused Charlie away from her as she gestured towards the bed. Tilley could only assume she was instructing him to lie down, perhaps even telling him to assume the position in a commanding tone. She watched as the attractive blonde woman used heavy silk ropes to tie Charlie Baker to the metal four-post bed frame. She watched the woman walk around to the side of the bed, and straddle Charlie's stomach. Knowing Marci Grant now, she understood why she had been attracted to Trudy. Trudy was an athletic, attractive woman and exactly Marci's type. She found herself feeling a little jealous as she watched the lithe blonde woman reach for a pillow.

Charlie's hands clenched and unclenched multiple times as his feet twitched as much as the rope would allow. The woman seemed to fidget some with the pillow held at chest height. She leaned forward, pressing the pillow on Charlie's face, leaning into it with all her weight applied to the pillow. Charlie bucked against the ropes. She watched Charlie struggle hard at first, weaken, and eventually stop struggling altogether. The blonde woman sat up, leaving the pillow on her victim's face. She seemed to hesitate there for a moment, as if already regretting her actions, Tilley assumed. She swung her leg backwards as she climbed off Charlie, knocking his manhood around in the process. Tilley watched it bob and weave with curiosity, but only for a moment. Trudy Wilkins had turned towards the rabbit eye camera, which recorded everything but sound. She watched as Trudy Wilkins picked up a thin, off-white blanket and draped it over Charlie Baker's torso. Why she did this, Trudy never said. It didn't really make sense to Tilley, but what she thought she saw was regret.

She watched Trudy gather clothes as she dressed, moving outside of the camera's view as she did. A few shadows were enough to show she was near the bed for a few brief moments. Shortly after, there was a flash of daylight as the front door opened and closed and Trudy Wilkins left the scene of the crime.

But the part that always bothered Tilley was that the camera kept recording for what felt like a while afterwards; a little more than twenty-two minutes to be precise. Much of which was a video of Charlie Baker's body tied to the bed. But as Tilley watched the video in its entirety for what was probably the sixth or maybe the seventh time, again she was disturbed when, near the end of the footage, Charlie Baker's foot moved. A few moments later, a brief flash of light from what had to be the door again; shadows appeared briefly and Charlie's foot moved again. Not long after, the video stopped recording. Trudy had gone back to retrieve the laptop computer.

Tilley sipped coffee and thought about her morning; about how Marci no longer wanted to sleep at her own house. She couldn't blame her. To find out your lover killed someone out of sheer jealousy would be hard enough to deal with, let alone having to be reminded of it every single day by still living in the same house filled with reminders. Still sleeping in the same bed you shared. It couldn't be easy. But six weeks of secretly dating wasn't enough for Tilley to take a leap and move in together. Three months of dating, maybe more, might have been enough to Dodge and Weatherbee, but Tilley was not the impulsive type. Not when it came to something as serious as living together. And yet Tilley hadn't felt so energized in her life. Marci Grant was electric, alive, and full of life. She had a zest for living that Tilley had never known, a passion that couldn't be satisfied. Tilley sometimes wondered if this was what Charlie Baker had been like; a man who just couldn't get enough, always wanting more. But Tilley figured all men had that dog in them, to a certain degree, of course. Some were great men, like her partner for instance. Turns out he was a one-woman man after all. He was in love and it suited him well, thought Tilley. But six weeks was too fast. It would take a long time for Tilley to want to live with Marci. Mind you, she could stay over often, thought Tilley, smiling to herself at the idea. That would be fine, for now.

Tilley quickly got up from her chair and set her coffee down. Her smile vanished as she fished through her desk for a set of keys and an electronic pass card. After a few locks and security card scans she was in the back storage where the evidence was stored. She located the boxes containing the Charlie Baker evidence. Scanning the listed contents of the boxes, it took a bit of time but she found the box she wanted. She used her key to tear through the tape on the box and opened it. The box contained some of the items taken from Charlie Baker's apartment. Tilley pulled out an evidence bag containing three smaller bags, each containing pill bottles, and smiled. The seals on the bags were broken, as she suspected they would be, and the pills were gone. Detective Tilley wondered who might have taken the pills. Was it Lemkie, Dodge, or most likely Calvin? Those were her first guesses, although many other men would have had access to the evidence room. She smiled, tucked the bag back into the box, and rifled through its other contents. She took another evidence bag, tore open the seal, and pocketed something before putting the bag back into the box and setting it back where she had found it. Tilley didn't bother resealing the box. The pill bottles alone were reason enough not to. She wasn't concerned about anyone knowing she had been in the box, nor would she tell anyone either. She glanced at the time on her phone as she left the station. If she had time, there was an errand she needed to run and as soon as possible, too. Just to be sure.

77

Marci Grant woke in Roxanne Tilley's bed, only to find she was alone as usual. She closed her eyes and ran her hand over the spot where Tilley would be if she was still in bed. Gone, just like every morning she had slept over. Tilley was an early riser, a genuine morning person. And just like all the other mornings, the coffee machine would be ready, her favourite cup with a single cube of sugar waiting for her. She'd shower and change at home, thought Marci as she collected her clothes which were scattered throughout the house. She finished dressing while brewing coffee, wearing a lazy smile of contentment. Clutching the warm mug in her brown-glove-covered hands and having had the first few sips of coffee, Marci decided she would start her day now. She went to her purse to find her phone to check for messages but instead found a small box with a silver bow on it protruding from her purse. On the box was a note:

These will match so much better.

The note was signed with a slanted drawing of a heart. Marci opened the box to find a brand new pair of fine black leather driving gloves. They looked almost identical to the battered brown ones she was wearing. She scooped one glove out of the box and touched it to her face. Real soft leather and not cheap imitation, this she could tell. She inhaled the aroma, a scent she loved. She hesitated for a moment and decided she wanted to make Tilley happy. She removed the battered brown leather gloves and examined them as if saying goodbye. The gloves had been a gift from the dealership where she had purchased her red Corvette; a car dealer who specialized in older model classics. She slipped on the new pair, caressed and smelled them. They were exquisite to say the least and must have cost a pretty penny. With her high-heeled shoe, which was completely inappropriate for the December weather, she stepped on the trashcan lever, opening it. About to toss in her old gloves, she paused. On top of an empty milk carton was a single brown button. Marci stared at it with a familiarity that made her skin crawl. She looked at her old brown gloves, one had a button and the other didn't. The button on the glove in her hand was identical to the one in the trashcan before her.

Did Tilley know? How long had she known? The button probably came off when she used the pillow to kill Charlie Baker. He was still alive when Trudy left, but Marci had a sudden opportunity thrust onto her to end the crazy jealousy and get rid of Trudy's insane obsession she called love once and for all. At the time, it was overwhelming and Marci had been struggling.

That morning, when she saw Trudy leaving Charlie's

place, she assumed the worst thing she could think of which was that Trudy was cheating on her. And in that moment, instead of anger Marci had a moment of what she would later think of as clarity. She had the sudden realization that Charlie had Trudy on film having sex, providing the perfect opportunity to be rid of her. Something she decided instantly that morning while at the Turlingtons', after seeing a panicked Trudy leave Charlie Baker's place. Only, it turned out they weren't just having sex. Trudy had tried to kill Charlie. She had realized that quickly when she entered Charlie's place through the unlocked front door. She had every intention of demanding the tape, but when she saw him on the bed with a pillow on his face she knew this wasn't just a sex tape. The video had captured a murder. But when his leg moved she realized Charlie wasn't dead. In a flash, she decided she would finish what Trudy had started as she proceeded to disconnect the laptop Charlie had told her about when helping her with her computer. This meant Trudy would be the one on tape, killing Charlie Baker.

Only, once the deed was done, Marci panicked. She had to take the video with her. Wrought with guilt, she found that she just couldn't go though with it. She loved Trudy, even if she was crazy. In a rash decision, she destroyed the laptop, or so she thought, and eventually got rid of it by throwing it out her car window. But there was no way she could expect Detective Roxanne Tilley to understand any of this. How did she figure it out? Her mistake had to have been locking the door as she left. She had done this without even thinking about it. As a real-estate agent, it was ingrained in her to lock up when leaving a client's house. That had to have been it, she thought as she stared at the button in the trash.

Marci was awoken from deep thought by the theme to Law and Order emanating from her purse. She retrieved her phone in a hurry and saw that she had gotten a text from Tilley. She had known who it was from by the special ring tone she had picked out just for her. She opened the text, hoping it was nothing bad.

Hey sexy, I hope you're not mad, it read. *I hope you like them, so you can throw out your old ones. See you tonight.*

Marci replied to the text.

I love them, thank you. They're very soft to the touch, just like you. See you tonight.

Tilley had to know. Marci couldn't remember when she had lost the button from the glove, but it was long ago, and the only way Tilley could have found it was if it was at Charlie Baker's place. But that message didn't seem like someone who was upset. On the contrary, thought Marci as she smiled, grabbed her things, and headed home to shower and change.

78

Standing before the dangling, pantyhose-clad body of the fire chief was a salt- and-pepper-haired senior Detective Franklin Dodge. The much younger Detective Roxanne Tilley just stared in disbelief. Both detectives had struggled with the smell when they first arrived on the scene but now were too shocked to notice it. Before them swayed the short, stocky body of the fire chief, suspended by a pair of pantyhose that had been used to make a noose. The chief's feet were bound together and his hands were bound behind his back, both with pantyhose used as rope. He was hanging from a partially pulled out hook in the ceiling; the heavy potted plant that used to be hung there had been tossed aside, smashing the pot and scattering its dirt as a result. The finishing touch was the multicoloured Christmas lights wrapped around the fire chief's body with a note.

Here's your Christmas bonus, you Fuck!

"What the hell does that mean?" Tilley asked.

Dodge sighed. "I don't have a clue."

"Did you call Lemkie?"

"Yup," Dodge replied. "But I left out the details. I wanted to see the look on his face when he sees this one."

"I heard Weatherbee got an offer on her house," Tilley said.

Dodge smiled, knowing full well Marci had told Tilley about it. "Yup, it's just about sold as long as they can agree on some of the finer details."

"That's great news," Tilley replied.

"Hey, how did you get the call about the chief here?" Dodge asked.

"Agatha called me," Tilley replied. "She got complaints from the tenants upstairs about a smell and finally got around to checking it out."

"Fuck me!" Lemkie exclaimed as he arrived, carrying his kit. "Just when I thought things were finally getting back to normal around here."

"This is normal," Dodge replied. "Around these parts, anyway."

Things were very normal, thought Tilley, who decided not to say anything to make anyone think otherwise.

"Emma and her Naughty Knitters are probably already spreading gossip about this as we speak. I need air," Tilley said.

"Me, too," Dodge added. They both headed outside, leaving Lemkie to get started.

The End

Author's note:

Book ideas come from different places for different writers. Mine tend to sprout from many places, depending on where my head is at. December 24th, 2015 I sat at my computer with an itch to start something new; but what to write? I had been told many times by people I knew that they didn't want to read my books as they didn't like scary stories. With that in mind, I decided to write something more light-hearted for a change, but I just needed to find the right topic. So I took inspiration from an image on a book cover that sat on a shelf in my office. The image was a set of handcuffs dangling from a bedpost. Now before you get thinking it was a smut book, let me say that it was *Gerald's Game* by Stephen King. Which turns out is an amazing book, by the way. But now with that image in my head, I wrote the opening scene for Poplar Falls and if you read this book before this note, then you might understand what I'm referring to.

This book has had many changes of titles over the thirteen months I worked on writing it. The story itself evolved many times before a plan started falling into place and it became what it is today.

As for the cover, I had an idea of what I wanted but sometimes you simply need to admit that others are just way better at some things than we are. So I supplied a professional graphics designer the picture I had taken and gave her a brief idea of what I was looking for. Soon after I found myself collecting my socks from across the room, as her work had blown them clear off. Figuratively speaking of course as this doesn't literally happen but I use this old adage to illustrate that she simply amazed me with her design skills. She took my suggestions but used her own magic to make this cover better than I had imagined it. The back cover author photo is by photographer Gerard Gaudet. The original front cover photo is taken by yours truly. The magic weaved to turn the plain photo into the amazing work that it is now, is due to the skills of Angella Cormier.

And with that said, I truly hope you've enjoyed this book and thank you for letting me entertain you with my story.

Sincerely
Pierre C. Arseneault